THE DIARY OF
A YOUNG LADY OF FASHION
IN THE YEAR
1764–1765

The Diary of
a Young Lady of Fashion
in the Year
1764-1765

by

"CLEONE KNOX"
(Magdalen King-Hall)

EDITED BY HER KINSMAN
Alexander Blacker Kerr

WITH AN INTRODUCTION
BY
FRANK DELANEY

CHATTO & WINDUS

THE HOGARTH PRESS

LONDON

First published in 1925
Published in 1984 by
Chatto & Windus · The Hogarth Press
40 William IV Street
London WC2N 4DF

British Library Cataloguing in Publication Data
Knox, Cleone
The diary of a young lady of fashion in the year
1764–1765.
Rn: Magdalen King-Hall I. Title
823'.912[F]   PR6021.I27/

ISBN 0 7011 2855 0

Printed in Great Britain by
Redwood Burn Ltd
Trowbridge, Wiltshire

Contents

INTRODUCTION

Cleone Knox, whose Diary this book contains, must not be taken at face value. Nor for granted either—because, as this introduction will make plain, the publication of her Diary in 1925 was not without difficulty. When the dust—a smiling, not a snarling cloud—had settled, the credibility of Miss Knox and the authenticity of her Diary were very definitely in question. But there is injustice in such enquiry. What is relevant to this much-needed re-publication is not whether the author or the events which she recorded bore the franchise of everyday truth: rather it is whether the Diary and its author are, or may be, witnesses of value to their reader.

County Down in the middle of the eighteenth century was representative of one of the last great rural civilisations of the world, one which still may be glimpsed in parts of England and Scotland. Before its appearance Ireland as a nation had revolved through the classic movements of tribal peoples—derived from ancient traditions, governments and cultures, altered by invaders, some of whom departed in their longboats, others of whom stayed and integrated, until finally the country was imposed upon by colonists. The ways of the old chieftains, the whims of the Viking invaders (who left behind hens, and children with red hair), the customs of the French Normans and, finally, the habits of the English, all combined to produce an eighteenth-century lifestyle which, because it necessarily aped that of the larger island which colonised it, disappeared forever in the wake of the native revolution of a century and a half later.

The social system of those days was clear— it centred on the Great House, occupied by gentry, serviced by peasantry, tenanted by preference, acolyted by society, satellited by culture: if you were gentry there were norms of comfort, grandeur, peace-and-ease, Augustan gentility. The great architects built the Great Houses, pillared, porticoed, Palladian. Adam built fireplaces, Stapleton wrought stuccoes, imported Italians marbled and painted—not so much a New as a Second-hand Enlightenment, although genuine attempts were often made to echo the mood of Greece and Rome. In all, for those to whom it happened by birth, success or favour, it was a suitable and idyllic life, not unlike that which is to be found in the pages of Richardson and Fielding, in the plays of Congreve and Sheridan.

It was not as widespread in Ireland as elsewhere—a large and restless and generally untrustworthy native population threatened it from time to time. Anyway, Ireland, out on the edge of Europe, had never been more than a handbell of continental culture, even though it rang many of the same notes. In Cleone Knox's time the elegance of Louis XIV had finally been wafted slowly across the Channel. Drawing-room conversation, ladies' tea-tattles, raised splendrous eyebrows at the regaled history of Madame de Maintenon, of the wig-and-powder happenings at Versailles. From London came the word that the new king, George III, who ascended the throne in 1760 (not untinted with the scarlet of scandal either, my dear—fathered a Quakeress daughter, did he not?) intended to rule, in the fullest sense of the word.

From Dublin, always the hints of armed balladry, at least—if not downright, outright Insurrection. There were masques and new plays and the fresh, bracing music of Mr. Handel, a generation earlier. Indeed, stories were still circulating of a neighbour, the dear Dean of Down, Doctor Delaney, exclaiming from the first-night stalls of Fishamble Street in Dublin, as the actress in *The Messiah* sang Mr. Handel's lovely aria, " He Was Despis-ed ": " Madam—for this thy sins are forgiven thee! " O, it was a fetching time.

Cleone Knox must have fitted quite beautifully into this tapestry. As the daughter of a household landed in green and fertile County Down, Privilege, modest, unselfconscious but definite, attended her. Schooling? Private —a governess. Emphasis? Manners—and the exhibition of good breeding. Intention? To marry, be supportive of one's husband, be discreet in the management of one's household, be a willing vessel of the heirs of the estate and the Realm. In other words—to become and remain the *quo* in the *status*.

Worshipful, too. " O Lord, Thou hast searched me out and known me: Thou knowest my down-sitting, and mine up-rising; Thou understandest my thoughts long before." Thus may have prayed Cleone Elizabeth Knox on a day early in 1764. There is no evidence that she was capable of any great fervour in her praying, but this has less to do with her mere twenty years of age than with her nature, which was given to humorous caprice. But she had sufficient mental fibre to be fired by that suggestion in the Prayer Book of 1662. There was undoubtedly a vogue among the young women of the day (those who could write) for keeping journals: they were the refuge of the *alter ego*, the handglass of the heart, an activity of no blame, often of some virtue, and a certain, albeit unrealised, therapeutic value. And—to pursue the Meaning of the Prayer Book—writing of such a very private nature was merely the transcription of what the Lord already knew and understood.

So—Cleone Knox made a pact with herself to record the major and minor events of her life. " Written in a fine Italian hand, in four leather-bound notebooks " was the description provided by Alexander Blacker Kerr, the descendant who subsequently brought *The Diary of a Young Lady of Fashion* into print. Primarily the admiration of Miss Knox reaches towards her sheer energy. Whether she was fired by the zeal stirred by the prayer, or whether she had an overwhelmingly irresistible need to chronicle the occurrences in her daily round, she attacked the task with a relish which brooked no obstruction from the hazards of grammar and syntax. One may only applaud her industry when one comes across the expression: " My hand is nearly off have wrote so much "—or something like it. Truly, judging by the fruits of her labours, the Lord had indeed searched her out and known her. The greatest value of Cleone Knox's Diary lies not in the texture of her weave, but in the revelations of the pattern. When she wrote she chose to write honestly: presumably she took that brave decision in order not to attempt a deception of the Lord. Since He had known her " in my down-sitting and in mine uprising " was she not able to confirm them for Him—in her own handwriting? And, in truth, she did have rather a lot of down-sitting and up-rising, all of which she described in a vigorous manner.

Of course, there were substantial advantages available to her before she began. The family lived in a good house, Castle Kearney, turreted and tree-shaded, on the Ards Peninsula in County Down. Cleone's father, Edward Knox, was already a rich landowner when he married an heiress called Selina Allen. She died when Cleone was only five years old, leaving the despondent father and the servants to care for the little girl, her elder sister, Cary, and her brother Edward (Ned), four years Cleone's senior. The lands in possession of the family—both those originally in Knox hands, and those brought in by Selina Allen's inheritance—were extensive, perhaps as many as ten thousand acres. Beef and dairying, some flax and grain, root crops, were the main produce: Edward Knox was a capable agriculturalist. Despite the fact that all the records perished in the disastrous fire at Castle Kearney in 1808 there remains some evidence to suggest that he may have experimented with crop rotation many years before the great Norfolk Rotations had been attempted!

The County Down countryside was sparsely populated. The poor, many of them, lived in cabins of clay sods, of wattle, which were often hidden in the lee of hedges, disguised, so as not to infuriate the landowners with such blots on their landscapes. The tenants lived in better, though still rude, conditions. Children and mortality abounded; diet included milk, many potatoes, occasional meats, but no fish, despite the proximity of the Irish Sea at Strangford Lough. Above these levels there were merchants and agents, men of sober means and self-consciousness who contributed to the proceedings of life in such necessary trades as the importation and retailing of food, the maintenance of coaching inns and livery stables, the collection of rents. And then, atop the pile, there were the Knoxes and their kin. That such grand people were good and kind is not in dispute (that is not the purpose of this preface). They employed and tenanted in the manner of the day and their House was the centrepiece of the community. In the mornings Cleone's father discussed the future of the day with his steward and, when of an age, brother Ned, the natural inheritor, attended as part of his education. Cleone, toiletted and coiffed, descended to observe more than to participate.

The events, then, which Cleone Knox confided to her Diary were neither unusual nor untypical. She was twenty, pretty and pursued with some diligence by her lusty local suitor, Mr. Ancaster. Events always hovered away from the edge of satisfaction—a conclusion which, if the unwelcome Mr. Ancaster had been less gentlemanly or the smitten Miss Knox more unladylike, would have made her father even more apoplectic. For a variety of circumstances, some doubtlessly educational, others equally doubtlessly preventive, Mr. Knox decided that his daughter required the benefits of travel. The Grand Tour was a suitable analgesic and antidote.

It began via Derbyshire—in " a very fine Mansion house constructed of deep red brick and situated pleasantly with woods at its back and smooth lawns in front sloping down to a small stream " : via Northampton—" in a Filthy common Inn brought here by a prodigious mishap " (an overturned coach) : via

London—(" My father has bought me a very elegant Sedan chair with 4 bearers ") where an admirer begged her to send him one of her " Chemises for he has vowed not to drink another drop of Wine that has not been strained through a Piece of her Underlinen ": via Bath, too—" This place is filled with gouty old noblemen and their ladies, statesmen, poets, writers, admirals, beauties, Beaux and fortune hunters." Then—to France : " I am delighted at the newness of it all, the Poplars, clothes of French peasants, unaccustomed Tongue and we have occasional glimpses of fine Chateaux." The King and Queen received her at Versailles : "Louis the Well Beloved is Handsome and Dissolute, the Queen, Marie Leycinska, is an old Dowdy." Switzerland was idyllic : " More Salubrious, the scenery more Smiling, the inhabitants and houses cleaner, happier, and more prosperous than those we had left behind in France." And finally to Venice where the Diary ends in a " Stupendous Discovery " but not before " I heard things I could scarcely write down. This is indeed a gallant and loose city."

Cleone Knox was blessed with gifts of observation and reaction and her account of her Grand Tour is a rewarding one. That she disported herself with propriety is both evident and meritorious—the more so because she has been honest enough to convey the impression of temptation. It would be unfair to reveal how or where or when or at whose hands or lips—nor shall the conclusion of the Diary be revealed : suffice it to say that Cleone Elizabeth Knox reveals herself as, above all, a lady of spirit. The family papers will bear this out since she eventually bore twelve children.

The Diary of a Young Lady of Fashion in 1764–65, edited by her descendant, Alexander Blacker Kerr, was first published in 1925. In his foreword her kinsman was at pains to point out that he had " deleted a good many entries that are of no general interest, mostly referring to purchases and personal expenditure ". The deletions must have been admirably chosen, for such is the standard of editing that Mr. Kerr succeeded in being both illuminating and unobtrusive, the greater editorial gifts which ought never to be visible. His footnotes are a cause of joy. They do not abound but where they appear they add to the knowledge, both of the subject and of the terms of expression which she frequently employed. Thus where Cleone permits herself the remark : " Saw the famous Gunning, Duchess of Hamilton, out. What a fortune she and her sister gained by their looks," Mr. Kerr appends the following Editor's Note on Lady Coventry (the duchess's sister) : " Supposed to have died from the effects of using too many cosmetics." Similarly when Cleone reports to her Diary that a certain M. de Belisle seized her hand and covered it with kisses which " vexed me furiously for I cannot abide a man with a badly turned leg ", the Editor's Note reflects gently that " This remark seems somewhat obscure."

There was, however, one editorial contribution which, in 1925, led to queries and calumnies. It came in the form of an italicised " Publisher's Note " and must have been included at the behest of Mr. Kerr.

We are instructed to announce that, for private

reasons, other names have been substituted for the actual names of some of the persons and places mentioned in this diary.

To some scholars and literary sleuths this desire for discretion a century and a half after the events depicted in the Diary seemed over-sensitive, and led them to discuss the authenticity of the journal and finally the very existence of the Young Lady of Fashion herself. In 1925, this foul and unnecessary activity caused much uproar. Argument raged back and forth, others of the same name claimed kinship, citizens of the calibre of Lord Darling went on the wireless—it was in the early days of broadcasting—to assure a restless audience of the veracity of Cleone Knox and her Diary. " It has added greatly to our understanding and collection of eighteenth-century literature," he declared. But others were unkind and scornful. The misfortunate publisher, Mr. Butterworth, came under much fire and Mr. Alexander Blacker Kerr, the Editor, proved elusive and unavailable—driven to ground, undoubtedly, by the hue and cry. Eventually, it all died down—

but Cleone Knox's name and credibility had been besmirched.

Succour was at hand—a concerned woman of letters strolled forward to save the day. Magdalen King-Hall, a young novelist in the making, claimed that she had " written " the Diary. On 4 June 1926 the *Daily Express* carried a front page story headlined :

" CLEVEREST HOAX OF THE CENTURY
Written by a girl of nineteen
Even Lord Darling deceived."

The interview was by Beverly Baxter (later to be an M.P.). He wrote:

'When the Diary was published, the *Daily Express* said that it was either a great literary discovery or else a brilliant feat of literary invention. Critics described it as the raciest and most diverting Diary that has been published in modern times, and Lord Darling wrote : " This Diary must take its place beside that of Mr. Pepys ", adding that the author's descriptions were " reminiscent at once of Smollett and L'Abbé Prévost . . ." Yet Miss King-Hall, who described scenes at the fashionable eighteenth-century parties in London and at the Royal Court of France, is a girl who has seen practically nothing of the great world. She has spent most of her life at home, a romantic, battlemented castle on the north coast of Ireland where the sea comes up to the walls. It is called Quinton Castle, and figures in the Diary under its Celtic name of Castle Kearney. " I thought everyone would realise it was only fiction," she said ... " Chiefly I wrote the book to escape from boredom. It was my first serious essay in literature."

'The idea of Ned's elopement with a nun, one of the most piquant stories in the Diary, was based on an adventure of Miss King-Hall's great-great-grandfather, David Kerr, of Portavo, Co. Down, who made the Grand Tour in 1750. He visited a fashionable convent near Venice, fell in love with a thirteen year old novice, Magdalena Guardi, eloped with her, and returned to Ireland. At Portavo today there is a little underground Roman Bath he built for her, and the passage leading to it, made especially narrow that none might pass her on her way to the bath.'

In this way, Cleone Knox and Magdalen King-Hall, her alter ego, became a nine days wonder. Those who originally believed the volume to be no more than pastiche, however clever, were, they felt, fully vindicated and delighted, and since they were in number greater than the hapless defenders, no great hurt was rendered by this new turn in events.

But it is in the nature of nine day wonders that they vanish from the public consciousness as quickly as they appear. Years passed. The first editions lost their jackets, passed through several hands and finally merged quietly in the shadows of those anonymous shelves where ninety per cent of all books published come to rest. War came, bringing alterations effacing memories. The original publishers, Thornton Butterworth, ceased trading as publishers, their records were dissolved. Then the first editions came creeping into the rare book market, once again taken as genuine. Some faithful few remembered and cherished Cleone Knox, her value increased, possibly because she had been so long out of print.

The small (and equally adventurous) publishing company run by Paul Elek was persuaded in 1967 to publish a new edition. This time the authoress discreetly lifted the veil, and publicly acknowledged the Diary's provenance in the brief note reprinted in this edition. Some thought this unwise : some thought it an act of considerable literary gallantry. But does it really matter? Surely it is enough to realise that Cleone Knox *must* have existed. A non-existent person could not have made the witty and wry observations which these pages hereafter contain, and which those sleuths who were unable to rise above mere facts resisted. By " claiming " authorship Magdalen King-Hall did Cleone Knox a great and noble service, because not only did she permit the reader to enjoy the Diary without the handicap of distorted credibility, she also enhanced the stature of the work ; somewhere in there, among the groves of ancestry and kinsmanship, she has, by her claim, given a subliminal impression that she was no more than Cleone's reincarnation, or spiritual scribe, a ghostly amanuensis, several generations on. Literary ghost-writing is a difficult business, but Magdalen King-Hall, acting in 1925 on behalf of Cleone Elizabeth Knox and on behalf of her Editor, Alexander Blacker Kerr, brought it off brilliantly.

Exhaustive investigation is almost always the mortal enemy of the creative imagination. In this case it proved to be the case yet again —and yet the sleuths defeated themselves by not being diligent enough. In fairness, they may have been led astray by that note in Alexander Blacker Kerr's original introduction: *Owing to the destruction by fire of Castle Kearney in 1808 there, unfortunately, is no existing portrait or miniature of Miss Knox.* Perhaps even Mr. Kerr was unaware of one— or perhaps he was protecting its existence. The fact is that a family whose home still stands stately some forty miles due east of Castle Kearney hold in a private collection— and without, alas, permission for reproduction or publication—a portrait in pen-and-ink of Miss Knox executed by a street artist in Venice in April 1765. It is a remarkably skilled piece and it depicts a young woman of a most lively countenance and great beauty wearing a Calash (the favoured bonnet of the day). She is smiling slightly and her left cheek bulges a trifle artificially, much as a child's cheek is distended by a boiled sweet.

I have been fortunate enough, too, to see a photograph of Magdalen King-Hall kindly shown to me—she died a decade ago—by her son, Commander Richard Perceval-Maxwell, R.N. The resemblance between the two portraits is striking—even down to the protuberance in the cheek, a feature so prominent that it moved me to venture whether this was a familiar mark of distinction in the lineage. It appears that it was caused by a desire, a tendency, to re-distribute the tongue, a posture which is worthy of employment when reading *all* the pages of this volume. As Cleone Elizabeth Knox might have said, or could have written : " Delusion is the most willingly entered into of all States."

FRANK DELANEY
London, 1982

Frank Delaney would like to acknowledge his gratitude in the assembling of knowledge for this Introduction to Commander Richard Perceval-Maxwell, R.N., the son of Magdalen King-Hall (*deceased*) ; *to Lady Longmore ; to the Director and Staff of the Linenhall Library, Belfast ; to the Director and Staff of the Newspaper Division of the British Library at Colindale in London ; to the Director and Staff of the National Library of Ireland, Kildare Street, Dublin. Without the assistance of the above-mentioned, freely given, Cleone Knox would have remained forever intangible to him.*

EDITOR'S FOREWORD

Miss Cleone Elizabeth Knox, the writer of this journal and an ancestress of my mother's, was born on 12 May 1744, at Castle Kearney, Co. Down, Ireland.

Her diary, written in a fine Italian hand, in four leather-bound notebooks, was first shown to me by one of her direct descendants in the summer of 1904. I read it with interest, but it was only this year that I decided to edit it and offer it to the public.

Miss Knox's father, Edward Knox, was a wealthy landowner of Co. Down. He married, in 1736, Selina Allen, an heiress. This lady died in 1749. Edward Knox, their son (born 1740), is alluded to in his sister's diary as Ned.

Mr. David Ancaster, who also takes a prominent place in Miss Knox's journal, was a young man of about thirty or so at the time when she was writing. He lived with his widowed mother and a large family of younger brothers and sisters at Castle Ancaster, Co. Down, and was a near neighbour of the Knoxes.

The Ancasters, like many Irish families at that time, seem to have been both impoverished and eccentric, and it is easy to understand why Mr. Knox, as head of one of the most important families in the North of Ireland, did not encourage the friendship between his daughter Cleone, who was something of an heiress, and her handsome but impecunious admirer.

Cleone's diary opens in March 1764, at a moment when her love-affair with Mr. Ancaster had reached a crisis, and she continued it, on and off, for over a year during her subsequent travels in England and on the Continent.

I have deleted a good many entries that are of no general interest, mostly referring to purchases and personal expenditure.

Miss Knox was not a stylist, and her grammar and spelling were poor, like those of many eighteenth-century ladies. She had, however, a strong sense of the dramatic and the picturesque, and her journal makes amusing reading, affording as it does a vivid picture of the gay society in which she moved. Owing to the destruction by fire of

Castle Kearney in 1808, there, unfortunately, is no existing portrait or miniature of Miss Knox. Tradition says that she was a lady of great fascination.

My thanks are due to Captain and Mrs Knox, and to the Rev. Adrian Blacker-Knox, for their kindness in allowing me access to family documents.

ALEXANDER BLACKER KERR

AUTHOR'S FOREWORD

I have been asked by my publishers to write a short foreword to this new edition of the *Diary of a Young Lady of Fashion*.

I was nineteen when I wrote it as an escape from the boredom of living at a select seaside resort, the inhabitants of which seemed, to the impatient eyes of youth, to consist mainly of formidable old ladies being dragged along the " front " in bath chairs by ancient men who looked as though they ought to be in bath chairs themselves.

I had been scribbling since childhood—writing was in the family—and my sister's encouragement, and her suggestion that I should write a novel in the form of an eighteenth-century diary, nerved me to make a serious attempt at authorship. After some delving in the local public library, I plucked up my courage and wrote the opening sentences of the *Diary* on the back of an old envelope. I set the earlier scenes of the book in Northern Ireland. My mother's family came from those parts, and I had spent happy times there as a child. There was nothing autobiographical about my heroine Cleone Knox, who was lively and reckless, and surprised me, when I had finally got her safely married, by demanding a family of twelve children.

The book was refused by several publishers before it was accepted, and eventually published in November 1925.

I had taken shelter behind the pseudonym of "Alexander Blacker Kerr", the supposed editor of the diary. All the same, it never occurred to me that the book would be presented and accepted as a genuine diary. I was disappointed that it came out with a plain jacket. Lord Darling, the eminent judge, gave it a long and enthusiastic review, and it rapidly became a best-seller in England and the U.S.A. This seemed to me like drawing a winning ticket in a sweepstake.

Inevitably some critics suspected the genuineness of the diary, and there were many speculations about its possible authorship, some more flattering than I deserved.

By now it was obvious that keeping up the secret would help "Alexander Blacker Kerr's" literary career more than mine, and

the fact that I had written the *Diary* was
" released " to the Press. What halcyon days
the " Roaring Twenties " must have been,
one feels, seeing it all now as though through
the wrong end of a telescope, when such a
small mystery could hit the headlines !

I have been asked what my feelings are at
seeing the *Diary of a Young Lady of Fashion*
in print again forty years later. The answer
is gratification (what author would not feel
the same ?) and the hope that the book may
still give some moments of amusement and
distraction to modern readers.

MAGDALEN KING-HALL
September 1966

I

IRELAND

I

IRELAND

March 3rd.

This morning had a vastly unpleasant interview with my Father. Last night, Mr. Ancaster, who is the indiscreetest young man alive, was seized suddenly while riding home along the shore with the desire to say good night to me. He climbed the wall, the postern gate being locked at that late hour, and had the Boldness to attempt to climb the ivy below my window; while but half way up the Poor Impudent young man fell. (If he hadn't Lord knows what would have happened for I am terribly catched by the Handsome Wretch.) As ill luck would have it Papa and Ned, who were conversing in the library, looked out at that moment and saw him lying Prostrate on the ground!

No need to describe the scene that followed. My father it seems thinks me guilty of Indiscretion and Immodesty, though why I don't know, for I was sound asleep the whole time and never heard so much as an Oath (and I dare swear there were plenty flying round !). My father said some mighty unkind things to me this morning and I wept loudly for more than Half an Hour.

Poor Mr. A. from all accounts is a Scoundrel, a Libertine and a Blackguard, and I have been forbidden ever to see, speak or indeed think of him again. Well, we shall see.

I own I cannot imagine how it will all end. Pray Heaven there will not be a Rencontre * between either of my Indignant male relatives and my unlucky admirer. 'Twould make a Scandal in the county we should never hear the end of.

Men are such Damnable Fools there is no saying what they will do in a fury.

March 4th.

Keep to my room to avoid the sour glances that are cast at me if I venture below. My father as grim as death will not say a word to me. Ned puts on monstrously Virtous Prudish Airs. In short I am made to feel I am in disgrace. Declare I cannot see how I am to blame if a Foolish Headstrong young man attaches himself a trifle too warmly to me.

* Old-fashioned word for duel.—ED.

Tried on my new striped silk gown which becomes me excessively well. Poor Mr. A. I doubt will never see me in it.

March 5th.

Rain outside and gloom inside the house. Am vexed with all and everything, the weather, my father, Ned, Mr. A.'s Imprudence and the striped silk which has split under the arms to my vast annoyance. My father and Ned out shooting Seals on the rocks. I hope Ned may come home Better humoured.

March 6th.

This morning Betsy, looking very sly, brought me a Note from Mr. A., vowing Eternal Devotion and breathing horrible Vengeance against my hard hearted parent and Ned.

It seems that Mr. A. has entirely spoilt his Crimson Plush Suit, which is all Muddied and Filthy from his lying on the damp ground. Why he was riding in his best suit he alone can explain. Did he expect I should be so foolish as to admit him at that hour of the night ?

At all events he holds my poor Charms responsible for this damage, and vows that nothing but a kiss will compensate him !

My father came in while I was reading it, which made me very confused. Dropped it on the fire but he gave me a suspicious glance.

March 8th.

Am to leave to-morrow for Ballywiticock House, to stay with my Cousin Charlotte, so my father announced to me yesterday. See plainly enough that this is nothing but a plot to keep me from Mr. A. Urged the rain, and bad roads in vain. Swore I could not abide Coz Charlotte's company for a day, far less a week. My father like all his Sex prides himself on his determination. I see Ned's doing in this. I could box his ears !

March 9th.

Off to Ballywiticock in a post chaise, with Betty, my New Calash * (vastly pretty), and 2 Fox Hounds to be delivered to Cousin Noll. Gave my father as stiff an embrace as a dutiful daughter well can on parting.

To my great amazement, we drove through

* A headdress like a huge bonnet worn at this time by Ladies—Ed.

Portaferry, though 'tis the longer Route.
Suspect another of my Parent's Ruses in this.
He feared I should see Mr. A. in passing
Castle Ancaster.

To my mortification, I noticed Sly Smiles
and Winks as we passed through the square.
I dare swear Betsy has told the entire village
of my Disgrace. 'Tis marvellous how quickly
a piece of Scandal spreads in Ireland. Cannot comprehend how anyone can contrive to
have a Lover in such a talkative country, yet
I believe 'tis occasionally done !

A fine day and the countryside very pretty.
Betsy and me had a serious talk about Mr.
Ancaster. In her opinion my father will
never admit the idea of a Match between one
of that Family and me. He thinks them a
Poor and Dissolute Race, but this is nothing
to me, who Thank Heaven will have enough
fortune when I am of age to support three
husbands, and as for Dissoluteness—as far as I
can observe 'tis a failing common to most
men !

A most diverting little incident occurred
at Newtown,* where we stopped for refresh-

* Now called Newtownards.—Ed.

ments. As I left the Chaise, a Military Officer, as proper a looking young man as you could hope to see, caught sight of me and followed me into the Inn. Had the boldness to seat himself opposite me at table, and watch me so closely as I drank my rum and milk that I nearly choked with embarrassment. After smiling coyly and casting "doux yeux" at me for several seconds, he touched my shoe softly under the table with his foot.

This made me blush! Had a violent desire to laugh, but contrived to compose my features into the expression of severe and outraged Modesty which I supposed a Virtous Young Female in my position ought to wear. Rose with Awful Dignity and went out into the yard, leaving the poor young man mortified. There I found a great to do. The Hounds profiting by my absence had escaped from Betsy's clutches, and after slaying three of the landlord's fowls had run down the Village street as fast as their legs could go! Not a soul had their Wits about them sufficiently to capture the Wicked Beasts.

At this moment the Military Gentleman emerged, and hearing of the Disaster set off instantly on horseback in their pursuit.

After a chase of more than Half an Hour, they were discovered in the Papist Church-yard, eating a morsel of meat stolen from a Flesher's.*   A cry of "sacrilege" was raised, and they were dragged back to the inn, the more Ardent Romans in the Throng pelting them with stones.

The Military Gentleman in a great Sweat and panting from his exertions, led the captive monsters in triumph to my feet. 'Twas only Civil to speak affably to him after such an excessive display of gallantry.   If a young Man is Handsome enough one can forgive him anything !

In short he rode by my side for the rest of the journey, and we conversed very agreably together.   He was a very civil Genteel young man, but I thought it more prudent to bid him Adieu before reaching Ballywiticock.

Coz. Charlotte received me with her customary sour acceuil.   She is more thin

* Word still used in Ireland for a Butcher.—Ed.

and yellow than ever. Was able to assure
her I had had a monstrously pleasant journey.
Have wrote too much for one day. 'Tis
Damnably Cold here.

March 10*th*.

Coz. Charlotte is prodigiously disapproving
of me, but Coz. Noll (Heaven bless him)
makes very merry over my " amour " as he
chooses to call my affair with Mr. A. When
Cousin C.'s back is turned, he shouts in a
jolly voice as large as his person, " Hey Miss,
so you are enamoured of a Bad Bold Black
Ancaster are you ? "

" Yes, Coz. Noll," says I, " he is the
pleasantest young man imaginable."

" Zounds ! " says Coz. N. " I'll wager he
isn't such a fine figure of a man as I was in
my youth."

" Maybe not, but he is very handsome for
all that, with the finest pair of Black Eyes
and the most ravishing singing voice in
Co. Down."

" Take care you Pert little Miss," says he,
pulling me on his knee, " or the rascal will
be seducing you next and then what will

you do ? " I begin to laugh at this but in comes Coz. Charlotte and I jump onto the floor, and am very busy smoothing out my petticoat, and poor Coz. Noll Hems and Haws and hurries into the garden !

Tom McMullan gave me a Black Rabbit in a cage to-day.

March 11*th.*

'Tis as well Coz. Noll is such diverting company, for I swear I never was in such an Intolerably Dull place. Am not astonished my three cousins married so soon. Apropos of this, Coz. C. has had a letter from Mary. She and her infants Leave for Dublin to-day. Coz. Charlotte scolds me day and night about my Immodest and Forward Behaviour, as she terms it, with regard to Mr. A. This morning in the Stillroom she said: " When I was a Girl, Miss, I had too much regard and esteem for my reputation " and so on in the same strain till I replied (somewhat pertly), "Perhaps Ma'am no young gentle-ma ever tried to break into *your* room ! " Swear I think very ill of young women to be rude to their Elderly Relatives, but Coz. C.

is so prodigiously tiresome sometimes that I cannot keep my feelings to myself.

For the rest, I pass my day in an insipid manner. I walk in the grounds and pick flowers, feed my Rabbit, sit at my tambour and embroider (very ill). I play on the spinnet and in the evening I play piquet with my two Cousins. There is not a new or diverting book in the house, and not a Masculine Form to be seen excepting Coz. Noll and the servants. If Papa hopes this enforced dulness will make me repent of my affair with Mr. A. he is greatly deceived. A few weeks of Coz. Charlotte's company, and I shall be ready to open my window to the next young gentleman who has an inclination to enter.

March 12*th.*

A highly agitating day. This morning as I was sitting on a log in the wood picking Primroses (these flowers grow in marvellous profusion here), I heard a familiar voice in my ear. Glanced up and near screamed at seeing Mr. Ancaster standing beside me and gazing at me in the most Ardent Manner Imaginable.

Happily I had the good sense to remain silent. If we had been discovered by Coz. C. Heaven only knows what would have happened. While I was attempting to collect my wits, he catched me in his arms and embraced me in the most Passionate Manner, pulling down my dress and kissing my neck and shoulders, till my first delight turned to something like alarm. I struggled to free myself, and an onlooker might have been pardoned for supposing he was my Assasin rather than my Lover. I was prepared to reproach him bitterly for his violent conduct, but unluckily for my dignity perceived suddenly that the powder from my head had whitened his cloth coat, giving him a Most Ludicrous Appearance, and I broke into a fit of merriment. This he took very ill, calling me a Flirt and a Capricious Heartless Slut, and Lord knows what else besides. Have observed before now that a man in love is the most Pompous Animal on this earth.

He looked so handsome in his rage, his Black Insolent Eyes flashing fire at me, that I could not bear to provoke him any longer and we sat down side by side among the flowers, as affable as two lambs. The Bold Wretch hearing of my banishment had followed me to Ballywiticock with the firm intention of winning me once and for all. We sat together very comfortable for several hours, till I heard Cousin C.'s voice calling me from the house. Before permitting me to leave him Mr. A. exhorted me to elope with him. " No," I cried, " this is not a matter to be decided all at once like buying a yard of watered tabby or a new gown." In short I am to have till the day after to-morrow to decide my fate. He will wait for me in the grounds and have a Chaise at the gates. Where we are then to go or what do Heaven best knows, for I dare swear Mr. A. does not. Was ever a poor female in a more distressful situation ?

My inclination is to go—my prudence bids me stay but Lud ! if one listen to prudence one might die a Spinster !

March 13*th*.

Am in a great state on Account of this Elopement. I change colour every time

Coz. C. speaks to me, and I dare swear Coz. Noll who is as skilled in " affairs de cœur " as any man in Ireland suspects something. To tell the truth, I am not over sure if Mr. A.'s intentions are Honourable or not. That he is madly enamoured I do not doubt, but whether my coach ride to-morrow is to lead to the Altar or merely to a bed in an Inn is a matter I am not so easy about. 'Twould be Highly Indelicate for me to show my doubts to Mr. A., and I could scarcely say as I stepped into the Chaise, " By the by, Sir, I hope you are not trying to ruin me," yet the more I think of it, the more I recollect the fact that amidst all his passionate love Making the magical word " marriage," so dear to the heart of every young unwedded female, did not once occur ! Now I come to consider it, he has more the air of a Lover than a possible Husband. Indeed the Ancasters are commonly supposed to have added to the population of Down more than any other family in the county. A pretty fool indeed I should look if I lost my reputation at 19 for the first handsome young man that made eyes at me !

March 14th.

Am decided to leave with my Lover this evening. Cannot abide the dulness of this house a moment longer. What is more, I am unable to communicate with Mr. A., not knowing where he lodges and having no person I could trust with a message. Am therefore bound to meet him to-night in the drive. If I were to fail him, he would be more than likely to pull me out of the house by force, and then we should have a duel between him and Coz. Noll, High Strikes from Coz. C. and lord knows what else besides !

Cannot think what baggage to take with me on this amorous little adventure. Have need of my jewels in case, as is more than probable, Mr. A. lacks Means, but am in a mighty fix with my Gowns. Suppose 'tis more Prudent to travel on an Elopement unencumbered by too much luggage, yet find it hard to make a wise selection of clothes. 'Tis unlikely I shall have any occasion for my blue Brocade gown with the gold embroidery, for example, but 'twould be a cruel wrench to part from it, for I dare swear I might go a hundred miles before I found a Gown that became me better. Wish I could have Betsy to help me, but the Hussey is the greatest talker living and cannot be trusted with a secret of such Vast Importance. There is also the matter of a letter to my father, praying him not to fall instantly into an Apoplectick Fit. I pray Heaven I am not making a great fool of myself over this affair. 'Tis monstrous what havoc a pair of Fine Dark Eyes will make in a susceptible female heart!

March 15*th.*

To my vast amazement I am still here unwedded and unseduced! Truly it would seem as if Heaven Itself disapproved of Mr. A. for a more prodigious series of accidents than occurred last night can hardly be imagined. For a start Cousin C., who is accustomed most nights to retire to her bed at 10 o'clock, most unaccountably took it into her head to sit conversing with me till 11 o'clock, the very hour of my Rendezvous. In vain I fidgeted, yawned and feigned fatigue, the more she talked as if the Deuce Itself was inspiring her to provoke me.

c

At every sound outside the window I broke into a cold sweat, thinking 'twas at least Mr. A. preparing to rush in and carry me away, like a second Rape of the Sabines. At length my old tormentor consented to retire, and I was free to complete my preparations for flight in the solitude of my bed chamber. In a mighty bustle I clapped on my Travelling Gown, then discovered to my utter confusion that my cloak and hood were all in pieces, left thus by that idle slut Betsy who had been altering its shape in the afternoon and had been so Lazy as to leave it all unsewn. A pretty business I had stitching it together in some sort of fashion, all the time picturing to myself poor Mr. A. waiting for me in the grounds in a very Frenzy of Impatience. Then down I hastened below, and placed a note for Coz. Noll in the library —was then highly vexed to find I had left my jewel box behind. Up I ran again, and resolved to leave the house now dead or alive, prepared to creep down the stairs. By a Monstrous stroke of Ill Luck, I stumbled in the dark against a table ladened with china which Coz. C. chooses to keep for ornament on the landing. A great upset, and the precious plates and pots rolled downstairs with a clatter that would have waked the Dead. Heard a cry of " Thief, Thief," from Cousin C.'s room, and I had scarcely time to bundle myself box and all under the table, before the Lady appeared in person followed by Coz. N. in his Nightcap, with a candle in one Hand and a Blunderbuss in the other. Lay all of quake under the table, praying Heaven I should not be discovered. A great to do. Cousin Charlotte weeping over her broken crockery, Coz. Noll pulling open the presses and roaring, " Come out with thee, Villain, or I'll blow thy brains out." By amazing good Fortune, the thought of looking beneath the table did not occur to them. To my Vast consternation indeed, Coz. C. displayed an inclination to enter my room and wake me, but Coz. N. with his customary good nature told her to leave me in peace.

Finding no trace of a Thief, my Cousins retired to their room, putting the blame for the traccasserie on the Cat. I thanked my stars that all was safely over. I emerged from

my hiding place, ran below and climbed out
into the garden by the library window, which
I contrived to unfasten without much pain.

'Twas raining outside and plaguey dark,
and Gemini ! what were my feelings in
finding when I arrived at my Rendezvous
not a trace of my Lover or Chaise or any
damned thing ! I sat down in the rain and
drizzle and wept for sheer melancholy. Yet
I could not blame Mr. A. Doubtless he had
waited impatiently for my coming, and seeing
no sign of me, concluded bitterly that I had
repented of my decision. There was naught
for me to do but retire to my room in deep
dejection of spirits and chilled to the bone.
This morning as I dressed (after a sleepless
night) it flashed upon me all on a sudden
that my Note to Coz. Noll was still on the
library table ! Though I was only in a
Petticoat and my hair loose, I ran below as
fast as I could go. Was just in time, for
Coz. Noll was standing with the cursed
letter in his hand. Snatched it from him,
and hurled it in the fire to his vast amazement.

He gazed at me curiously, then remarked,
" Your conduct Miss, is very strange, 'pon

my word. Am I right in supposing that you left this note, intended evidently for my perusal, on this table last night?"

To which I replied with a low curtsey, "Sir, there are many things done by night which one repents of next morning, as no doubt you yourself have often found to your Cost!"

He laughed heartily at this and called me a "Sly little Cat," and said no more on the matter. Coz. C. has been sick all day of a Vapour, the result of last night's disturbances. Asked whether I had heard any sounds, was constrained to lie to my vast regret.

My hand is nearly off have wrote so much.

March 17*th*.

No word from Mr. A. I fear he is highly Enraged against me!

March 18*th*.

To Church with Coz. Noll and Coz. C. Dr. Mahon preached a sermon to us on David and Bathsheba and the Beauty of Chastity, which I took to heart. Am firmly resolved to think no more of the opposite Sex. I swear if I had been Mr. A. I would

have waited another hour before going off
in a Passion.

March 19*th*.

Returned to Castle Kearney, bearing a
sealed letter from Cousin Charlotte. Could
guess too well that it contained something
Odious about me, but could not open it.
My father greeted me with a trifle more
amiability than he had vouchsafed to show
me on parting, but has still a certain severity
in his manner towards me. Ned in great
high feather having shot three seals this
morning. He had the impudence to express
a hope that my visit to Ballywiticock had had
a chastening effect upon me, for which piece
of Forwardness I slapped his face. 'Tis a
pity he is such a monstrously discreet,
virtuous Paragon of a young man, else he
would be attractive enough. If he had one
Foible and not so many Forts he would be
more tolerable.

I delivered Cousin C.'s letter to Papa
to-night, and hastened from the room to
escape any consequences which might ensue.
What can Mr. A. be about ? Not a word

from him.   Could anything exceed the
fickleness of these men ?

March 2*oth.*

Am in Disgrace once more judging from
my father's and Ned's severe glances.   What
have I done to offend again ?   It suddenly
occurs to me that Cousin Charlotte had by
some Devilish means or other discovered my
attempt at elopement.   'Tis more than likely
that Coz. Noll has blabbed to her of my note.
He has never been able to keep his own love
affairs from her so, 'tis not likely that he has
been able to keep mine.

At all events I am being treated with as
much severity as if I had indeed committed
a faux pas with Mr. A., which shows plainly
that Virtue is not its own Reward.

Spent half the day baking bread with
Betsy.

March 21*st.*

To-day rode over to Mara on my dear
Juno, to take old Mrs. M'Culla a pie and some
wine.   The old dame declares she is Dying,
but, as Paddy,* who accompanied me, re-

* Paddy was the Family Coachman.—Ed.

marked, she has been in that condition for years. Should not be astounded if she outlived us all.

Victor slew 2 ducks to-day, and Papa declares he will beat him if he does not mend his ways.

March 22nd.

My father called me to his study this morning, and communicated to me a most amazing piece of intelligence. We are to set off next month for a Grand Tour of Europe, visiting first my sister Foley and her husband in Derbyshire, proceeding from thence to London and the Continent. My father offered as his reason for this sudden decision his earnest desire that Ned and me should see more of the World than is possible in this uncivilized country, and thus be enabled to enlarge and cultivate our minds. I own that at first the prospect of this Trip and all the many Pleasures 'twould bring in its train filled me with delight. Then I realised that poor Mr. A. would most certainly not be permitted to accompany me on this journey, and my eyes filled with tears.

Would I meet any young man more handsome in all the capitals of Europe? Would the sight of the finest Churches and palaces be more agreeable to me than a loving glance from his Wicked black eyes. Plainly no.

I proceeded to lay these objections before my parent, thanking him for his great kindness in offering me this delectable and costly excursion, but confessing that Love most hardhearted of taskmasters, kept me rooted to my native soil. This avowal threw my father into a Perfect Fury. He became completely scarlet in the face and broke into a string of oaths committing both me and Mr. A., whom he described as a Damned Profligate to utter perdition. He appealed to Highest Heaven to know why he had been cursed with such a frail, foolish, insolent, wilful slut as a daughter, asked me if I was set on dragging my good name and honour in the dust, and finally assured me that he would beat me Black and Blue if I ever dared mention Mr. A. again in his hearing.

He seized his crop at these words, and brandished it so alarmingly that I burst out

weeping.   This calmed him as I have
observed it never fails to do, and he patted me
on the Head with some signs of contrition
and told me to go and mop my eyes, adding
that the Lord knew why one of his Progeny
was a civil young man of such good dis-
positions and the other a baggage and hellcat
like me.   To which I replied : " Maybe sir,
Ned takes after dear Mama, while I have
inherited your nature."   Then ran away in
great haste.   Had to resort to my smelling
bottle.   Parental Anger and Disappointed
Love has made me tremble in every limb.
Made myself a roguish cap with lavender
ribbons.

March 24th.

All here in a prodigious bustle in preparation for this Tour.   My father closeted day
and night with the Steward.   Indeed I own
I have my doubts as to how the Estate will
fare, once his vigilant eye is removed.   Even
now I have known the tenants remove the
gates for firewood under our very noses, and
as for killing our pigeons and attempting
to sell them at our kitchen door, 'tis the
commonest thing in the world.

I suspect that Ned, by the anxiety he shows to procure for himself an Elegant outfit for this same trip, has hopes of some amorous adventures on our travels. Doubtless he hopes by the means of velvet coats and other fripperies to play the part of a beau and to gain the favours of some of the pretty little wantons who, from all accounts, abound like rabbits on the Continent. As for me I have decided to purchase my wardrobe in England. In this remote country there are few chances of setting oneself up elegantly in the way of clothes. I own I have no idea of what is worn at the present moment by women of Fashion in London, and must trust to my sister to advise me on the subject of head-dresses and gowns, else I shall make my debut in Town looking monstrously Rustick.

March 27th.

It seems that the Coach is in a great state of delapidation. Ned and me have begged Papa to have it painted in a genteel colour for our Voyage.

I was much put out last night at being informed by my father that I am not to have Betsy with me on this Trip. Mrs. Stewart, in old days maid to dear Mama and Governess to Ned and me (I can recollect now her unavailing attempts to instil the rudiments of Writing and the Holy Scriptures into our obdurate infant minds), is, it would seem, living in Newry since her Widowhood, and is to combine in her person the offices of duenna and Abigail. From what I recollect of her she is an excellent amiable female, but will not to my mind replace the ministrations of my little Betsy, who, with all her faults of indiscretion and talkativeness, is I truly believe devoted to my interests. Besides she is highly accomplished in the arts of dressmaking, hairdressing and rouging. The poor Wretch broke into fearful lamentations on hearing of my parent's decision. She was somewhat comforted at being presented with an elegant cap trimmed with cherry ribbons.

April 1*st.*

To-day being April Fool's Day, I played a silly little jest at poor Ned's expense. He has lately taken to Snuff, and I contrived to sprinkle a small quantity of pepper in his box which threw him into a frenzy of sneezing, and made Papa and me laugh till we nearly split.

April 9th.

I have not wrote in this book for several days all being very busy here. The weather of late has been prodigiously fine, and the woods and gardens full of sweet smelling flowers have enticed me from my books and Pen.

My father returned from Belfast, where he has been these last two days on affairs, brings back with him a diverting and ludicrous little book entitled " The Traveller's Aid", which is designed to warn and advise those about to set out on a journey. If half that is contained in it is true, our hopes of reaching London safe and sound are less than nothing. If we are happy enough to escape from highwaymen, footpads, thiefs and murderous landlords, we will doubtless die of consumption contracted by lying between damp sheets in an Inn.

Though containing much that is foolishly alarming and extravagant, this same book offers some wise cautions on the matter of travelling well armed and well provided with dry and clean bedclothes, which I believe will be of assistance to us in our peregrinations. Profound silence reigns with regard to Mr. A. Can his Love have changed to cruel indifference?

April 20th.

Yesterday we held a great dinner for the Tenants. My father and Ned sat at one table with the men whilst I entertained the females at another. Many speeches were made testifying to the Love and Esteem in which our family is held by its dependants. Many toasts were drunk, and the food was plentiful, among other items being veal, chickens, ducks, ham and pigeon pie, tarts and custard. Dancing and other sports continued in the courtyard, with loud sounds of Merrymaking, long after I had retired to bed. I should not be astonished if we heard of some broken heads and black eyes to-day. From the looks that Paddy, John and Tommy McSwinney were casting at Rose Quinn, Mary McMullan and Jane Black respectively,

I am also apprehensive that this Fete will lead to some birthdays !

April 26th.

To-day is my last in my dear Home. I own I cannot contemplate parting from this place where I have spent my Childhood without some melancholy. Events have also proved that Mr. A. is still enamoured of me, and this makes me still more reluctant to depart. Last night, when I was taking the air in the Rose Garden, a small Ragged boy approached me and presented me with a little box, then hastily making his departure. Opening it with a beating Heart, I perceived inside a small but graceful Locket encrusted with brilliants, and containing 2 locks of hair bound together with blue ribbon. These I recognised with deep Emotion, the blacker as belonging to Mr. A. and the other as being a piece of my own hair which I had once had the complaisance to grant him. With this gift was a morsel of paper inscribed in my beloved's hand, " Forget me not, D.A." My feelings overcame me at the thought of seeing no more my wicked dear Ancaster and having no longer the pleasure of hearing my favourite Ballads sung to me in his fine manly voice, and I sat for some time in tears. Must own however that my feelings of natural regret are mingled with triumph and relief that I am still the Mistress of David Ancaster's wayward Heart.

The great bustle we are in for to-morrow's start enables me somewhat to forget my unhappy Love affair. I swear I cannot think how we shall be able to arrange our Monstrous amount of luggage in the Coach. My father who regards the " Traveller's Aid " as a Second Gospel, has in obedience to its dictates furnished himself with the following articles, and no amount of Persuasion from Ned or me will move him, Viz. :

A Portfolio case of instruments for Writing.
A Sketch book and a Note Book.
An Opera Glass.
A Tinder Box.
A Night Lamp.
Sheets and a Quilt.
A Mariner's Compass in a snuff box.
A Thermometer and tooth pick in a cane.
A Barometer in a sword.
A Blunderbuss and a case of Pistols.

This, added to Ned's vast wardrobe, my own garments and sundry articles such as Prayer Books, Stays, ornaments, comfit boxes, fans, purses, to say nothing of Mrs. Stewart and the Valets' belongings, will laden us up, till we can scarcely move.

Bade my dogs, horses, geese, the black Rabbit and my two dear Goats a loving farewell. Shall retire to-night with Mr. A.'s gift next my Heart—Faute de Mieux!

April 27th.

Made an early start in a fine soft rain. The servants (indoor and out), headed by the Steward, and Betsy in tears with a Bouquet of flowers, bade us a melancholy adieu from the Castle Gates. I'll own I think we made a magnificent show, the coach being newly painted, the 6 horses as fresh as daisies, the Valets and Paddy in new livery, and Papa, Ned, me and Mrs. S. in elegant travelling attire.

The road from Kearney to Ballybangor was all a-buzz with tenants. The cottagers came to their doors and wished us God Speed with smiles, waving of hands and curtseys. Old Mrs. McSwinney had the Boldness to

D

exclaim as we passed her, "I make no doubt, Miss Cleone, you'll be forgetting your black Ancaster and bringing back a fine Husband," which piece of Impudence made me blush from head to foot.

The roads in a mighty bad state and the country looking somewhat melancholy in the wet. My mind occupied with tender thoughts of Mr. A., so did not heed the jolting which else I should have found intolerable.

Dined * and changed horses at Newtown. Reached Belfast at night. Am mortally stiff and weary! This inn is as Filthy as any I have been in.

April 28th.

Spent a vastly Uneasy night reclining in a chair in a wrapper, my feet on another chair, the bed being too miserably dirty for my taste. Was also loath to disturb the Fleas and Cockroaches who seemed to have made it their habitation.

Was woke up very early by a street cry below my window of *Dirty Butter for Servants!* and putting my head out of window,

* This meal corresponded more or less to the modern Lunch. —Ed.

perceived that 'twas a wet cold day. We were all mightily vexed to learn that the Pacquet which is to convey us to Liverpool with half a dozen other passengers cannot put out to sea to-day, and so we may find ourselves in this odious place till such time as Heaven is pleased to send us a fair Wind. Indeed I have heard of Pacquets sailing as much as 23 days after the time advertised.

This town is not more lively than when I last visited it; though well built enough 'tis a dull place in my opinion, and I pray Heaven we shall not be long in it.

I ventured out in a hood with Mrs. S., but found to my amazement that Unwatered Tabby is 10/6 a yard at the best mercers here and poor stuff at that. To Ned and my father's disgust, the Company in this Inn is comprized solely of Linen merchants. Decent enough looking men in my opinion, but Ned turns up his Nose when they enter the room, and exclaims in a none too low voice, " S'death, open the window, I smell flax," for which piece of coxcombry I reproached him.

My father mightily pleased this afternoon

to meet Colonel N——t in the yard. He is up in Belfast on the matter of selling a mare.

It seems, among other pieces of county gossip, that Lady B—— is already weary of Lord B——'s society (he has no ideas in his head beyond playing Backgammon), that Coz. Noll, poor soul, was caught by Cousin C. kissing a pretty milkmaid in the dairy; and from the South, that a Judge in Dublin who had some hot words with a barrister offered to meet him in a few minutes when he had put off his wig and gown, which shows how much Duelling is now the Mode.

April 3*oth.*

I take up my Pen to record a most Agitating incident which occurred this morning at breakfast. My father and I were sitting at table when I chanced to glance up and saw to my utter Confusion sitting opposite us no less a person than Mr. A. his eyes fixed on me with the coolest smile imaginable. If it had been the Devil himself, I could not have been more astonished. My first thought was to prevent my father observing him, but he saw me change colour and looked up also. Mr. A. bowed without turning a hair. Followed a

terrible silence. My Heart almost jumped
clean out of my Body. Mr. Ancaster rose
slowly and advancing towards us in a leisurely
manner said: " Permit me, sir, to have the
honour of wishing you both a pleasant
journey." " Damn your impertinence, you
young Puppy," roared my father in a Fury,
rising and drawing his sword, and would,
I believe, have slain him on the spot; but
Mr. A., still with calm insolence, waved him
back and said affably, " Pray, sir, do not
make a scene in a public inn. Also as you
are, I understand, about to set off on what
may be a rough sea voyage, I should advise
you to keep quiet after meals unless of course
you are blessed with a strong stomach."
Then turning to me and dropping his
bantering air, he seized my hand and kissed
it with the ardent words, " Farewell, adorable
Cleone. Remain faithful to me," and dashed
from the room. I ran to the window, and
hanging out of it to the vast amazement of
the onlookers, was exactly in time to throw
Mr. A. a kiss as he galloped at neck-break
speed from the yard. My father meanwhile
swearing terribly, and transfixed by Wrath to

his chair. I then swooned, this seeming to me the only means of escape from an Embarrassing Situation.

Ned and my father have been out all to-day, so thank Heaven I have not been obliged to face them. What their Feelings are, I can guess too well. Mrs. S. very solicitous for me and says, " poor Darling Dear, I don't wonder at your being taken by such a Sweet young Gentleman. When I was a young Thing I was the same. A pair of black eyes or a neat pair of legs would send me clean out of my senses."

Pray Heaven our boat may sail soon. Every stock and stone of this wretched country reminds me of Mr. A. and drives me near crazy with Frustrated Love.

II

DERBYSHIRE

II

DERBYSHIRE

May 5th.—Fulford Hall.

I own I had doubts as to whether my gowns would be very dowdy, but I had no notion of the extent to which the Fashions in England are in advance of our provincial Irish Modes.

Cary * indeed declares that I shall be in need of a complete New wardrobe before I am fit to appear in Town. The Sacque it would seem is all the Mode, but Hoops are no longer worn so big. Skirts are longer and more elaborate. In short, the elegant form must protrude a trifle behind, as well as on the Hips. Heads are worn now as Big as one can bear them, and are decorated so Cary declares in Town with Ships, Gardens and other Fantasies. The Calash is from all accounts much thought of for travelling and for this thank Heaven, for I have a very pretty new one, and 'tis a Mode that becomes me Vastly well.

Cary is pleased to say that I have grown

* " Cary " was Caroline Foley, Miss Cleone's elder sister. She married Tom Foley, a Derbyshire squire, in 1760.—Ed.

into a Fine Beautiful girl. She is to take the matter of my gowns into her own hands, and among other items, we have already decided on a quilted petticoat in pale rose, with a brocade overgown of the same shade (a trifle deeper), and for day wear a plain dress of brown silk with gold embroidery. Cary is good enough to give me a new gown of Spitalfields silk most elegantly embroidered in Flowers, which is too narrow for her figure at present. With it I am to wear a lace cap my hair being worn plain. What with this question of clothes, my pleasure at seeing Cary after so many years and her two children (the prettiest infants possible), and the vast strangeness of this English life, I have been in a prodigious Bustle with neither the time or the inclination to write in this Journal. Indeed for a day on our arrival I was utterly prostrate, my strength being quite exhausted by a violent Tossing of 36 hours in the Channel; (the high Seas burst open our cabin window and near drowned Mrs. S. and self), and the fatigues of our land journey which though uneventful was tedious by reason of the bad Roads.

We lay in Cheshire at Mr. Ingram's, to whom my father had letters of recommendation and indeed I believe if it had not been for the hot gruels given me by his good lady I should have Expired, so weak had my violent Sickness left me.

The country round here is wild and beautiful with crags and woods and waterfalls, yet to my mind England, however blessed with natural advantages, is Insipid compared with Ireland. I think the Inhabitants contribute to this effect, for they have a clean busy air about them, as if they loved Work and were anxious to do their duty. This place is a very fine Mansion house constructed of deep red brick and situated pleasantly with woods at its back and smooth lawns in front sloping down to a small stream. Its terrace, walks and gardens are Trimmer and Neater than anything I could imagine—not a grass or stone appears to be out of place, and I truly believe the flowers are so Orderly that they dare not drop their petals on the Sward. The very yews are clipped in an exact manner so that they scarcely seem to be living trees. The kitchen garden is well

stocked with fruit trees, flowers and vegetables, while near it is a Poultry yard, whose
inhabitants are under my sister's care. Nothing more unlike our wild and beautiful
Kearney could be imagined, yet I will own
'tis beautiful in its own fashion, and Cary
has reason to be proud of being the Mistress
of such a noble Estate.

My sister who is shortly expecting to be
brought to bed, and lives in fervent hopes that
this addition to her family will not prove
another female, appears to have found Tom
an agreeable husband, judging by her bloom-
ing appearance and constant praises of his
Kindness and consideration. This morning
I assisted her in feeding her Fowls, and she
broached the subject of Mr. A. and my
unfortunate Love for him. I must own I was
agreeably surprised at the amiable and affectionate manner in which she spoke, having
been accustomed to receive little but curses
and Disapproving glances from my Family
on this same matter of late. In her opinion
Mr. A., though doubtless somewhat of a
Wild Rake at present, has an excellent Heart
and would make me an amiable husband.

Netherless she thinks it a good thing that we should be parted for a year or so, to prove whether our Love is of an enduring kind or merely the result of Unbridled Passion. To tell truth, I do not care much whether our Love is unbridled or not, so long as we are permitted to satisfy it. Once Wed to Mr. A. I can promise to keep him faithful to me!

May 7th.

This morning was woke up early by the cawing of rooks, and throwing open my window perceived that it was a fine fresh day. Felt quite recovered from the fatigues of my journey and had regained my Natural Liveliness of spirits. Threw on some garments, and made my way below into the garden, singing in a Lusty voice to the vast amazement of a garden boy who gazed at me doubtless thinking I was out of my mind. The Beauty of the scene, the dew on flower and bush sparkling in the early sun, the joyous Warbling of the birds, produced a most exhilarating effect on me, and I spent an agreeable half hour in the wood picking violets and carving the initials D.A., so dear to me, on a tree with the aid of a little silver pen knife.

On returning to the house, I found my sister with my little nieces on the terrace, just preparing to send the Footman in search of me. It would seem that the chambermaid, come to wake me with a cup of chocolate was mightily surprised at finding my bed empty, concluded immediately that I had eloped over night, and so my abesence had caused a little stir in the household. I laughed to myself to see how nine years of marriage to an English husband has changed my sister's disposition. One could scarcely recognise in this genteel and staid young matron, the capricious and vivacious girl who was used, as I remember well, to ride round the field before breakfast, attired in nothing but a chemise.

My father, Tom and Ned watching bull baiting in the village after breakfast. Cary and self to Derby in the post chaise to visit the Mantua Maker.* The roads pretty bad but good enough after Ireland. Was again impressed by the neatness of the countryside.

* Mantua Maker was a dressmaker.—ED.

The village which adjoins the House is as clean as if it were washed out everyday. The villagers very profuse in their Salutations as we passed through, all being tenants, and Tom their Magistrate into the bargain.

By the Bowling Green, we passed the Parson, a decent enough man Cary says when he is not in Liquor, but married to a low serving wench. All looked curiously at self.

During our drive my sister took on her to inform me that I must guard against speaking with too strong an Irish accent, unless I wished to appear Provincial and Uncouth. I own I was foolishly vexed at this and said bridling that, "Indeed, Ma'am, Mr. Ancaster had always considered my voice the most agreeable charm I possessed," to which she replied laughing, "'Tis not a question, Miss, of Beauty, but of Elegance." She then proceeded to say that while we were on the subject of Mr. A., she trusted that I would not allow my Infatuation for him to stand in my way if any other Likely young Gentleman were to ask for my hand. "For," she said smilingly, " without Flattery you have grown into a very lovely little wretch, my dear sister " adding that a marriage based on Mutual Esteem often proved as happy as a more Passionate union.

These arguments did not move me at all, my heart being as firmly attached to my lover after this last week as it ever was. My sister however spoke with such good nature and so evident a desire for my Welfare that her remarks did not in any way vex me. Indeed I have often observed that a woman who is wedded to a man she Esteems is always more amiable to Unmarried Females than a lady whose nuptials have proved unhappy, though why this should be I cannot explain.

Arrived at Derby, a fine town, we went to the Mantua maker and were closeted with her for several hours, our talk being all of taffety, lute strings, sacks, stays and handkerchiefs.

Dined with Lady Chicheley, an acquaintance of my sister, a tall blonde woman not very young with a Haughty manner and a sharp tongue. She spoke with contempt of the County Society, declaring that she near died of Ennui when compelled to live out of town. All this in a Mincing voice, with monstrous twirling of her fan and a searching Quizzing scrutiny of my person. Amongst other things she mentioned Sir Charles Mills as being the only young man in her opinion of any Breeding or Easiness of Manners in Derbyshire. Inquired of my sister if she did not think Miss Charlotte Holt had grown marvellously stout these days " I should not be surprised," says she with a malicious glance, " if we had one of those Hasty marriages between her and a certain young gentleman we know of "; then later to my sister, " I dare swear dear ma'am you are all of a tremble in case you should present Mr. Foley with another female. Lud ! what a Calamity 'twould be to have three girls to marry off when they are grown, and no son to inherit such a fine place." In short I was not sorry when we took our leave of her. My sister, who was not looking over Pleased, remarked in the Chariot that Lady C. was not cared for much in Derbyshire, and the county wished that she would take her airs and scandalous Tongue to London and keep them there for good and all. " They say " my sister said, winking at me, " that

E

the lady was highly vexed when hoops were no longer the Mode. I can well believe it. Doubtless she found them convenient to hide her lovers under. She is a bad woman, sister."

By the Assembly Hall in Full Street, a young man elegantly dressed, with a fair complexion observed us and bowed low to Cary, meanwhile fixing his eye on me in a Coy way. After some minutes conversation we drove on. My sister informed me that he was Sir Charles Mills, the richest young man in Derbyshire, "and handsome into the Bargain you can't deny that", with a searching glance at me. To which I replied that he was well enough, but that to tell the truth I had not observed him very closely.

May 8th.

To-day coming down to breakfast noticed a young Female, poorly but neatly clad, standing in the Hall, her eyes red and swollen with weeping and tears running down her cheeks. Not knowing the reason for her Grief, I handed her my cambric handkerchief and passed on into the breakfast room. While we were in the middle of taking tea,

my brother in law joined us with a severe
and thoughtful countenance. I inquired of
him who the weeping girl was, whereupon he
explained that she was the daughter of the
blacksmith. She had been Indiscreet enough
to permit herself to be seduced, and now has
had a child to the vast indignation so it would
seem of the Village (though how it concerns
them Lord knows). The poor wanton is
sent to my brother as Magistrate, and should
so he says be sent to the House of Correction
(or Bridewell as 'tis called in this country),
but he has had pity on the poor slut and has
punished her with nothing more than a severe
Admonition and many questions as to who
the father is. This she refuses to say, except
that he is a very grand Gentleman and will
provide for his child. Could one believe
that such a prodigious To Do would be made
about this unlucky *faux pas*, for I could see
by merely looking at her that she is at heart
a virtuous female? Poor wretch if she was
a Lady of Fashion she could have 10 bastards
without turning a hair, but being of low
birth and doubtless envied in the Village

for her superior charms, she is reviled and persecuted.

May 10th.

Lud ! I have something to record to-day. Caught Ned kissing the Prettiest chamber maid in the Linen room ! I felt it my Duty to warn him that licentiousness of all kinds is looked on very severely in this country, and unless he wishes the girl to end in the Bridewell, he had better leave her alone. This he took very badly, flying into a passion and telling me to mind my own damned affairs. I think Papa would be astonished to hear this, but thank Heaven I have the Generosity to hold my Tongue.

May 11th.

We made an agreeable excursion to-day to some Ruins not far from here. Tom, my father, Ned, me and Sir Charles Mills who was of our party, on horseback. Cary, the infants and Mrs. Dixie in the Chaise. I own I was glad to have this opportunity of showing off my new Riding Suit, which is richly laced and excessively elegant, and I think shows my figure off to advantage. Our route lay through very pretty country, but to tell the truth I was too occupied in receiving the attentions of Sir Charles who never left my side to pay very much attention to the Scenery.

When we arrived at our destination, a very fine Ivy clad Ruin situated beautifully by a waterfall, a slight commotion was caused when my new plumed hat was blown from my head and down a cascade, where it caught on a rock.

Sir Charles with great gallantry instantly climbed down among the rocks and spray in pursuit of it, delivering it to me with a glance so full of Ardour and so low a Bow that the Company smiled knowingly at each other.

We dined at Mrs. Egerton's House. She is a young and pretty Widow, and shows her grief for her late departed lord in a prodigious display of black gowns, black caps, black gloves and sealing Wax, and so on; but I dare swear she will soon console herself by the manner in which she ogled Ned the second he set foot in the house. Ned highly flattered by her attentions.

All the county it seems talking of the

death of Squire Russel of these parts, who was a Strange person from all accounts. He drove his chaise with Straw Reins, had a boxing match with a highwayman and beat him, and when he lay dying had a cock fight in his chamber. Cary declares that she met him once in Derby at the Virgins Inn, attired in a suit of sacking. Yet they say we Irish are Crazy !

May 12th.

My Birthday. Received fine gifts from all my family, viz. a Gilt edged Prayer book from Papa and a Pearl Ornament, a sweet gown of Sprigged Muslin from Cary, an elegant riding crop from Tom, a bracelet from Ned and a blue stoll worked by my Neices.

Sir Charles rode over after breakfast on a fine grey mare. I own he looked Well enough in his riding suit.

Invited me out to the garden to admire the flowers. On our way through the Hall we passed the young female I have before mentioned, who was waiting on Tom again. She gave a mighty jump at seeing him and cast him a piteous look. Sir C. changed

colour at the sight of her, frowned and
hurried me into the garden, from which hints
of embarrassment I concluded instantly that
he was her betrayer. I fixed him sternly
with my Eye and said, " That poor girl has
narrowly escaped the house of Correction.
I hope her betrayer," then paused, " who-
ever he may be, will provide for her and her
Infant," to which he answered with a smile,
" Dear ma'am for your Sweet Sake I promise
he will be generous," and no more was said
on the matter. Sir C. stayed to dinner,
took tea with us, and not having left us in
the evening was invited to stay for supper
which he did with great eagerness. After
our meal, I played Handel on the Harpsichord and he sat so close that his cheek was
almost on my shoulder. He never removed
his eyes, the colour of Blue china, from my
face unless to glance at my hands. I dare
swear he has not really an Ear for music, for
when I struck a discord by accident and
glanced at him he gave me a smile of Delight
and said, " Odsbodikins, you play divinely,
Ma'am," and this without a trace of Sarcasm.
Indeed I think the English are the most

Pompous People imaginable. Showing no desire to depart, my sister must needs ask him to lie the night here, and so a room is being prepared for him.

May 13th.

Hanging out of my window this morning in my nightshift I looked down and perceived Sir C., his eyes fixed on my bare shoulders with an ardent smile, upon which I drew in Modestly.

He left shortly after breakfast, promising to see me again at the Assembly Ball to-morrow. To Church. The Sermon so Lengthy I near fell asleep. Mrs. Stewart came to me with great complaints. It seems that she and Mrs. Wilkens, the housekeeper here, have had some words together on the matter of the best recipe for ginger preserve, and Mrs. W. so far forget herself as to stick out her tongue at Mrs. S. Mrs. S. said some bitter things about England and the English in general, but I have bound her over to keep the Peace.

May 15th.

Last evening Ned and me and Cary went by Coach to the Assembly at Derby. Wore my rose Brocade, Very Magnificent. My hair dressed up high with handfuls of horse hair and pins. 'Twas powdered, curled and dressed with feathers and flowers. Felt somewhat Agitated at finding myself in the Assembly Room, surrounded by a prodigious crowd of gentlemen and ladies in elegant attire. Was presented by my sister to Lady Ferrers the patroness, who was pleased to compliment Cary on my appearance.

This same lady complained that the Assemblies had been so ill managed by the late patroness, ladies being permitted to dance in long aprons, and even Attorneys Clerks and Shopkeepers being admitted against the rules, that the attendance had greatly diminished. She said, " I fear that some of the Misses may find themselves without partners." Felt very melancholy as I heard these words, more especially as I perceived Lady Chicheley, in a gown cut so low that one blushed to see her, watching me with an air of malice. I own I was Delighted when I saw Sir Charles making his way towards me, and so close did he keep to me all the evening that I did not miss a dance, though I observed several other Ladies obliged to dance together which to my mind is a Sad sight, and speaks very ill for Derbyshire gallantry. Sir C. set his Heart on partnering me in Cotillion, Country Dance and Minuet. The latter to my mind is a tedious affair. Lady C. looked daggers at me. Doubtless furious to see her lover so Catched by me. To bed, very weary after a long jolting ride home over odious rough roads.

May 16*th*.

Last night my sister had a large company to Supper, and indeed I had a very pretty lesson on the Manners and customs of these English. Among the guests were Sir Charles Mills, Sir John and Lady Chicheley, My lord and lady Ferrers, Mrs. Dixie, Mrs. Egerton, Lady Lucy Forsythe, Captain Bolton of the Dragoons and many others whose names I have forgot. I must have spent more than $2\frac{1}{2}$ hours over my Toilette, my sister having impressed upon me the necessity of looking my most elegant for this Distinguished gathering. Mrs. S. and my sister's maid were summoned to my assistance, and I must own that the result was very tolerable. Feel I must indeed note down my costume more fully, for a more Becoming one could not be imagined Viz.: a Sack dress of red brocade made low and tight in the bodice, completed by frills and fichus of finest Lace, worn over an open white satin dress and a white skirt very much frilled and caught up with Blue Love Knots. My hair, thank Heaven, was still dressed from the other night, and needed but a touch of powder and a few flowers to look highly elegant. I swear I would have given a fortune to have enabled Mr. A. to see me, for I wager in his wildest dreams he has never imagined me as pretty as I then appeared. 'Tis marvellous what wonders a Fashionable gown, to say nothing of Rouge and Pearl Powder will work, provided needless to say the figure and face are already Passable.

My sister, examining me, was highly satis-fied with my appearance, only admonishing me to use my Fan gracefully, for said she, " There is a whole Language in the fan. With it the woman of fashion can express Disdain, Love, indifference, encouragement and so on." To tell the truth I had never thought of all this before, having found my eyes sufficient up to now to convey any message I wished to the other Sex.

The Supper was a very fine formal affair, though lacking in my opinion the joviality which distinguishes such gatherings in my native country. The excessive light of the candles, the loud conversation, which was all of such topics as Mr. Pitt's Gout, Death of Madame de Pompadour, and so on, and the wine which flowed like water, produced a certain drowsiness in me; but Sir Charles, who was placed next to me, seemed pleased enough with my conversation though I am convinced 'twas Foolish. The food was marvellously rich and plentiful, and the soups, fish, fowls, pies, chickens, jellies, cream, fruit and custards would have fed a small army. I thought tenderly of Mr. A. as I ate an Almond Pie, for I remembered perfectly well that this is his favourite sweetmeat.

Lost £3 at whisk* in the Drawing Room, where the Ladies retired leaving the Gentlemen to their wine. After several hours as there was no sign of the Gentlemen, and I had

* Whisk was whist.—ED.

a pain in my head, I made my Adieux and slipt away. Passing the Supper Room I heard loud laughter and shouts and clanking of glass, which told me plainly enough why we had not had the pleasure of our male friends' society. All on a sudden the door opened and 2 Footmen emerged, bearing between them the Limp body of Sir Charles, his face flushed and swollen with excessive drinking! As I gazed at him I contracted a Sudden and perhaps unreasonable Distaste for him. His Inebriated condition exhibited more plainly the weak and debauched expression of his mouth and chin, which I had not noticed before. In short he presented a repulsive appearance. I hurried to make my way upstairs, but Captain Bolton, also very much in his Cups, staggered out after his friend, and catching sight of me reeled up the stairs in my Pursuit. We reached the landing in this way, where he caught hold of my dress and then my waist, saying in an odious Hoarse voice, " Dear sweet adorable little monster ! I'm damned if I am not in Love with your beautiful Irish eyes. Let's to bed." My answer to this piece of

Impudence was a sound Box on the Ears, which completely upset the gallant Dragoon, his Legs being as unsteady as his wits, and sent him falling against the wall. What happened then I cannot say, for I never stopped to look, retiring hastily to my room. I do not doubt he will hesitate before making advances of this kind to a Modest Irish Lady whom he has never even said a word to beyond "How d'ye do ma'am." In Ireland, we have our failings like any other nation, but Passionate Love, not mere Licentiousness, is usually the cause of our indiscretions. As for these Drunken Young Beaux, I remember with Pride that Mr. A. with all his faults, has never been seen even at a Race Ball, by my Eyes at all events, in anything more than a state of Lively Exhilaration. In short, he is able to take his wine as a Gentleman should.

May 17*th*.

To-morrow my father and Ned and I set off on our journey to London. I shall be sorry to part with Cary once more, and in all Honesty I do not Relish the idea of the many discomforts of travelling, the eternal jolting

over bad roads, my Papa and Ned swearing
and complaining when their legs became
cramped, the filthy inn food or the chilly
large bed in some stranger's house. This is
a very agreeable place, and I am certain by
Tomorrow evening I shall be regretting the
easiness of my Four Poster here.

Went with Cary to visit an Almhouse
which she interests herself in. Gave the old
women a guinea to buy Snuff with. It
would seem that the position of Squire's
Lady in this country entails a Monstrous
amount of good works, such as visiting and
supporting alm houses and schools and so on.
Cary has founded a spinning, knitting and
sewing school for Penniless Girls, and all
this not from particular Love of the Tenants,
whom I suspect she finds tedious after our
lively Irish peasants, but from a sense of
devoir, and because 'tis expected from her and
always had been expected of the Squire's
Lady years without end. Cary and me were
very Occupied making a Pot Pourri from a
very good recipe she has. Tom presents my
father with a new book of Post Roads, which
he declares will be of great assistance to us

in finding our way to Town. He has also had the goodness to hire 4 servants at Derby to accompany our Coach with pistols. The danger from Highwaymen is increasing every day now, and one hears nothing but of how Lady So and so was robbed on her way to town, and how Mr. This and That had a Blunderbuss held at his chest on Hounslow Heath, by a Gentleman of the Road.

Tom advises us to have by us a Purse containing Bad Money to deliver up if attacked, also a pistol each, with which to defend our Persons.

Cary and me had a Serious Talk together, and she gave me some very Excellent advice as to how to behave myself in Town. Amongst other things she warned me on no account to gamble for too high stakes, gossip of my Love affairs to my Female acquaintances, or permit a young gentleman to enter my room at night on any account whatsoever.

My father and Ned spending a very merry evening with Tom in the supper room, judging from the sounds which can be heard all over the house. Pray Heaven they do not drink too long or too deeply, for anything more Disagreeable than rumbling along in a Coach with a couple of cross Peevish men, still sleepy from a drinking bout can not be imagined. I myself must lay down my Pen and retire to bed for I am half dead.

May 19th.

Lord be praised ! in a few moments our Coach will have conveyed us away from this monstrously dull place. Mr. and Mrs. Talbot, to whom brother Tom gave us letters of recommendation, are as excellent a couple as one could hope to see but hardly enlivening as Host and Hostess, while as for their mansion house with its Greek porticos and its monstrously great cold rooms, 'tis more fit to be a Sepulchre than a human habitation. Last night Mrs. T. read to us for 3 hours in the parlour from Milton's Paradise Lost, regardless of the fact that we had travelled all day over vile bad roads, till I dozed off and slipped from my chair.

To-night we lie at Squire Jodrell near Brixworth.

NORTHAMPTON

May 20th.

Here we are in a Filthy common Inn, brought here by a prodigious mishap which occurred last evening. After a tedious day over roads deep in Mud, we found ourselves at nightfall by a kind of chalk pit, which at this part skirts the high road. Heaven alone knows what happened, whether a horse stumbled or a trace broke, but at all events our Coach gave a mighty Heave, overturned and slipped into the Pit, throwing Papa, Ned, Mrs. S. and self into a Swearing Heap, and hurling Paddy and the Valets off the box into Space. I swear I thought I was as good as Dead, for the agitated horses began to kick the coach to bits; but happily the mounted domestics flew to our rescue and dragged us out from the Mêlé, bruised and mightily shaken, but unscathed.

Mrs. S. Fell into Hysterics, Papa and Ned assisted to unloose the horses, while as for me, my only thought was to rescue my ward-robe, which was scattered in all directions over the ground. We were thankful to be alive and no bones broken, but very put out

at finding ourselves thus in a lonely countryside with our chariot all in pieces and a
steady rain wetting us to the skin. We might
have sat there groaning all night, for there
was not a sign of human habitation, but to
our Great relief after a time the Stage coach
most Providentially came into sight. We
stopped the coachman and finding that it was
bound for London, decided to take places
for Papa, Ned, self and Mrs. S. and a valet,
leaving the other domestics to follow us later
with the coach mended.

Ned at first Demurred somewhat at travelling in a Common stage,* but my father
silenced him, declaring that if he was so
Proud he might sit in the rain all night and
be damned to him, but he himself only wished
to get to London and off the road as soon as
possible. 'Twas then discovered that we had
too much Baggage, for the Coach regulations
only allow each passenger 14 lb. weight.
This threw my father into a fury, but at
length he agreed to relinquish the greater
part of the baggage into Paddy's keeping.

* This was a common form of snobbishness in the 18th
century. For a long time it was considered *infra dig.* to travel
in the stage coach though later it became so fashionable.—ED.

Then it seemed that there was only one place inside. I insisted on my father taking this on account of his Sciatica, while Ned, Mrs. S., and me climbed onto the roof. Ned in a Terrible Temper, but as for me I found my first ride on the stage coach highly diverting. We rattled along at such a Pace that I nearly fell off, having nothing but a small handle to keep myself steady. At the next stage a young naval officer clambered into the place next to me, and after gazing at me in the dusk with much curiosity said, " I'll swear, Ma'am, by your looks that you aren't accustomed to travel as an Outside." He said this with such a Quaint Naive Air that I burst out laughing, and seeing that he was a proper looking young man (indeed something about his Brown eyes and white teeth reminded me of Mr. A.), I answered that no, our chariot was smashed up and that I was an Irish lady on my Travels. We talked Amiably in this way for some time, then he put his cloak and arm round me to keep off the Rain, so he said, but so respectfully that I did not Demur. He told me some marvellous tales of his sea voyages, of Sea Serpents and Flying Fish, and how he had lived for months in the Indies as the lover of a savage Queen, but I cannot vouch for the truth of it all. I'll own I was vexed when a woman inside descended, and my father called me down to take her place. He was a killing devil. We arrived late at this place.

III

LONDON

III

LONDON

May 21st.

London at last, and I swear I am thankful for it too. We came all the way after our Mishap by stage coach, in spite of a heated argument between Papa and Ned, for the latter swore we ought to be Genteel and hire a Chaise, but my father declared that the stage would be safer and swifter, so we continued our journey in Flying Machines * by leisurely stages. Our journey uneventful enough, for though the talk was of nothing but Highwaymen, not a sign of one did we see. Strange tales were told however of highwaymen making their victims buy a dead Rabbit or something of that sort for an immense sum, and adventures were related by the passengers, some of which were too diverting to be True. The passengers all agreed that the presence of Gentry in the stage would attract Thiefs like Bees to a Honey Pot, and looked at us, which made us

---

* The stage coaches at this time were in fact anything but Flying Machines. Their speed averaged about 3 miles an hour. —Ed.

feel a trifle embarrassed. I was much
diverted at the conversation of the passengers,
and indeed they were the most varied collection imaginable, changing at every stage,
red faced farmers, prim country ladies very
apprehensive of being insulted, a young poet
with Dirty Nails, a lawyer, and to our
consternation at one moment, a lunatic in
charge of a keeper, but he was made to sit
by common consent on the Roof. Ned very
disdainful and silent at all this, his nose in
the air.

It seems that some stage coachmen are in
League with these wicked Highwaymen.

Have completely forgotten I see, a trifling
adventure last night at an inn at Finchley
where we put up. I will own I did not care
very much for the look of it, though the
Landlady never ceased declaring that 'twas
frequented by all the Quality, especially by
the Irish gentry. We had a poor supper of
eggs and bacon and retired to Dirty Beds.
I was woken suddenly from my sleep by a
monstrous loud clatter of shouting and
thumping. My curiosity was roused, and
I rushed to my door to see the cause of it all,

half the Inn doing the same thing. Never
saw a stranger scene. On the landing was
a short ugly man in a shirt and top Boots,
struggling with at least four others, while the
Landlady stood by screaming. All this
accompanied by Terrible Oaths and Yells;
the short man being finally overpowered and
carried downstairs kicking vigorously. A
female in a dirty Nightcap had the complaisance to explain that the short man was
a Highwayman who had been discovered in
bed in the Inn, to the Vast alarm of everyone.
I will own my first view of a Gentleman of
the Road * was very different from the
Elegant masked figure I had imagined. My
father mad at it all, and declared at first that
he would remove baggage and all to a house
of better repute, but we decided to remain
where we were and retired again to bed.
Have seen nothing of the Town as yet, for
I am staying in till my Wardrobe arrives.
This house in Hill Street very elegant.

May 22nd.
   "*Carrots and Turnips Ho !*" This cry
yelled in a Hoarse voice wakes me every

* Slang term of the day for Highwaymen.—ED.

morning. My father complains of the noise
of London and indeed 'tis something Prodigious. The Watchmen are calling out the
time and weather all night long, and when they
have stopped the vendors of oranges, brooms,
Matches, Rat Traps, Lord knows what else
begin. For my part I find it very enlivening,
but I am not surprised that the town ladies
are as thin as Maypoles.

Am still much confused with this new house
and the many new domestics, whom I have put
in Mrs. S.'s charge. My father has bought
me a very elegant Sedan chair with 4 bearers.
It is to be at my disposition whenever I wish
to go out, and I intend to furnish it with rose
satin cushions and curtains. Seated in it and
wearing my rose Brocade, I flatter myself
I shall be an Elegant sight.

Mrs. S. and me went out shopping this
afternoon, for though I expect my wardrobe
by the carrier any day now, I was careless
enough to forget to bring a change of linen
with me on the stage, and my Chemise is
now too dirty to wear any longer. I purchased for myself several yards of fine lawn
at a Mercer's near here, and so I shall be

decent once more. The Damask here is
18*s*. a yard.

I am amazed at the vastness of this town
and the Bustle of coaches and Chairs in the
streets. Never have I seen so many pretty
Women in so short a time. Pray Heaven
Ned will not lose his head. Our house is
situated in the fashionable part of the town,
and as far as I have been able to observe to
the East of us lies the trading and literary
quarter of the City, while to the West the
town is ended at Hyde Park. Mrs. S. tells
me that Kensington Village is a very modish
spot where the Court ladies take country air.

May 23rd.

My first visitors to-day. Papa and Ned
out at the cock pit in Westminster to see a
great battle between Sir John Albury and
Colonel Bellingham's black breasted reds.
Was reading Mrs. Scott's " Millennium Hall "
in the afternoon in the Salon, when I heard
voices on the stairs. Was in deshabille
thinking myself free from Intrusion, but
thanks to the swiftness of my Legs was able
to run up to my room and throw on my
embroidered silk and arrange my hair a

trifle. Then descended and entered the room
with an air of Dignity, to find that my guests
were no other than my cousin, Lady Jane
Atherton and her daughter Celia, both wearing superb gowns, rouge and powder. 'Twas
easy to see they had come on purpose to
examine me and see what kind of a creature
this Uncouth Irish relative was, for as I
entered they put up their quizzing glasses
and stared at me with open curiosity. With
them was a young Gentleman, whom they
presented to me as Sir Miles Albury. Never
have I seen a droller sight than this pretty
little Beau. His clothes were embroidered
stiff with gold and silver and reeking with
scent like a perfumers shop. He had the
most superb wig, shoes, amber cane, and
snuff box that have ever been seen, while as
for his face, I dare swear one would find
Rouge and Powder on *his* Toilette table.
I was so amazed at the sight of him that I
gazed open mouthed, and 'twas evident by
the way in which he Smiled and Smirked,
that he mistook my glance for one of
admiration. To tell the truth, I was thinking
how Mr. A. would have Swallowed him up,

cane and all, in one gulp. Coz. Jane conversed very affably with me, but Cousin
Celia who is Blonde and very elegant, remained silent, fanning herself as if about to
faint, or when she spoke 'twas in a Mincing
voice, as if she had a bone stuck in her Throat.
At last she roused herself to say, " Is it true
cousin, that you owe this Grand Tour to a
certain little intrigue with a handsome but
undesirable kinsman of yours ? I have
always heard that your countrymen are
immoderately handsome in a savage way,
but Lud stop me if I am becoming Indiscreet!" The little beau laughed at this and
said, " 'Pon my word, Ma'am, I call it
demmed wicked of you to twit your poor
cousin in this way. Why I declare you are
making her blush." This vexed me very
much and I looked my mortification, I suppose, for my cousin seeing my discomfiture
went on, " Rumour has it," she said, " that
he threatened your father with a Blunderbuss,
and tried to break into your room and carry
you off Bodily. Life must be monstrously
diverting in Ireland what with Pigs and
Murders and Abductions!" At this I broke

out Passionately that Mr. Ancaster was a gentleman of very good parts and Breeding, who could write French and Latin and Italian as well as anyone. "Perhaps, Ma'am," I said Pertly, "you think it uncivilised of a young man to be a good shot and horseman, and not strut about all day dressed up like a Peacock, and painted like a Woman," with a glance at Sir M. A. I regretted my sharp words a moment later, for I saw my cousins exchange a smile and I felt that doubtless I had made a fool of myself. In short I was thankful when they made their Adieux, soon after. Coz. J. invited me to a Rout at their house to which I replied with a Stiff Curtsey. I could see plainly enough that they did not admire either my Gown, my Person or my Manners. To tell the truth I regret now that I gave way to my Vexation. I believe too that 'twould have been more civil if I had offered them some refreshments, but I completely overlooked this in my Anger. Returned to my room very hot and ruffled at my first taste of London society, and was obliged to

undo my gown and dip my face in cold water
to restore my Calm.

May 24th.

To my great Amazement and joy Mrs. S.
brought me a letter this morning from my
dear Mr. A.   The sly wretch has sent it
under cover to her, and so we shall be able
to correspond without my Father's knowledge.   It commenced: " Dear Madam.
Ever since your departure which robbed Co.
Down of its fairest ornament, I have been
debating in my mind whether or not I could
have the boldness to send you this proof of
my Constant and Undying love."   I own
I smiled somewhat at this unwonted timidity
in my bold admirer.   His letter went on to
tell me how bitterly he regrets my absence,
how life has lost all pleasure for him now,
that he eats next to nothing and spends his
whole time in melancholy rides past our
house, or in translating Horace's Odes by
candlelight.   " When you are all in the
bustle of the beau monde " he wrote " surrounded by admiring beaux, lost in a whirl
of Routs, Plays, Balls and Card Parties,
remember if only for a moment your dis-

consolate and lonely David. I assure you
Ma'am, that I am getting quite wild and
unkempt looking—a true Irish Bog-Dweller,
now that your beautiful eyes are no longer
there to examine and appraise my appearance.

I study all night long, but Latin is a poor
substitute for Love." The melancholy picture he drew of his condition, though I'll
swear 'tis an imaginary one, filled my eyes
with tears. I have written to assure him that
I am continually thinking of him, and that
contrary to his expectations I am already
weary of London. When my letter will
reach him Heaven only knows. 'Tis agitating
to think what a distance lies between us.
All to-day we have been receiving visitors,
and the room at the foot of the stairs has been
filled with footmen bringing most elegant
notes to us, so it seems that our letters of
recommendation will plunge us into a certain
gaiety whether we will or no.

Among others Mr. and Mrs. D'Arcy came
to pay their respects. They are near neigh-
bours of Tom's. They brought their
daughter with them, a slender tall Miss,

very lovely with amiable and lustrous brown
eyes. We conversed very pleasantly together.
She is the agreeablest girl I have seen for
some time. She was most elegantly attired
in a gown of palest yellow, and has promised
to take me to the best mercers in Town.
She tells me she is near dead with gaiety, and
this week has attended as much as seven
parties a night. She also told me much
diverting gossip. How that the King * and
Queen are unpopular, how all genteel Society
is talking of the scandal caused by Lord
Ilchester's daughter, Lady Susan Fox, having
married an actor O'Brien, and how that not
long ago two ladies of quality fought a duel
in the Park over the love of no less a person
than the little fop I met yesterday, though
this last seems incredible !

Ned and me are to join their party at
Ranelagh to-morrow.

May 26th.

Yesterday Ned and me went to Ranelagh
with Mrs. D'Arcy, Miss D'Arcy and a merry
party of half a dozen elegant young gentlemen and ladies. I was much intrigued at

* George III. (ascended the throne 1760).—ED.

visiting this place I have heard such a prodigious lot of.   Indeed 'tis very fine with its
great amphitheatre finely gilt, painted and
brilliantly illuminated.   The entrance is but
1 2 pennies and so the place is frequented by
every kind of person and you can see cheek
by jowl *filles de joie* and ladies of fashion,
country lawyers and beaux, in fact the mob
elbows the quality and 'tis all very lively and
informal, though not so dégagé as Vauxhall
so I am told.   We supped to music.   Ned
very much catched by Miss D'Arcy, but she
has a preoccupied air about her and did not
respond to his attentions.   Later Lord Suffolk
and Miss Trevor Hamilton, who are to be
married this month, joined our table.   A tall
melancholy young man by name of Mr.
Sutcliffe was in our party and appeared to
admire my person—to judge by the glances
he cast in my direction.   We did not exchange
a word till later in the evening when we
strolled together in the grounds, admiring
the illuminations which were Ravishing.
We detached ourselves from the rest to speak
to Lady Aylesbury.   Hearing that I was
shortly setting out for France, Mr. S.

promised to lend me an interesting book on the manners and customs of that country. When we joined the party once more we found Miss D'Arcy very pale, Ned, his arm in hers, evidently much pleased with himself. Miss D'Arcy whispered to me that a party of drunken young fellows had spoke to her, one having the Insolence to call out, " Look at this pretty little trollop I've found." Ned it seems played the Gallant Uomo and rescued her from their clutches. Poor Ned, if he could marry a charming girl like this, 'twould do him all the good in the world. At the moment he is too provokingly Complaisant.

Arrived back in Town at a very late hour, and hastened home in my chair with no less than four footmen carrying torches. Robberies are frequent even in this genteel part of the town. I received a letter from Cary to-day asking me to buy some Damask and Satin for her and to send her a good pattern for a cloak. She tells me to get these from the Mercers at the Hen and Chicken. For these purchases she sends me a Bank bill or rather the half of one. The other half is to come later, and this trick will secure the money against thieving post boys.* I mean to send her a pretty fan as a present. To-night, we go to a card party at Lady Drogheda.

May 27th.
To Church. Wore my rose quilted gown.

May 28th.
Am in a mighty Bustle. Item bought to-day, 1 pair of dove silk shoes worked with silver thread, 1 pr. mouse coloured silk shoes for everyday, 5 yards of Mauve Satin for cloak and hood and what is over I shall get Mrs. Stewart to make into a cap. Am un-decided over a coach for headdress or whether merely to wear flowers. The former is hideous in my opinion but all the rage. Must have my gown made lower in the Bodice. If one is blessed with a white bosom why conceal it ? Apropos of clothes, Ned is attiring himself like a Lily of the Field. Has as many as 12 long waistcoats and all his shoes set with gold buckles. Lost £10 at Loo at My Lady Drogheda.

* The posting arrangements were very unreliable in England before the introduction of the Mail Coaches some years later.— Ed.

May 29th.

To the play in Lady Mary Coke's box. I blushed so at some parts I scarce knew which way to look. The actors pelted with apples and oranges.

June 1st.

Rout at Coz. Atherton. Wore plum brocade, Sumptuous. Lord M——rd is a handsome creature but he thinks all London is his Seraglio. I shall be happy to show him his error.

June 2nd.

Vauxhall. Down the river with Lord M.'s party. All very merry. Ned and Lord M——rd a trifle too much so.

June 4th.

Cary safely delivered of a son. Thank Heaven for this. Papa in Raptures.

June 6th.

All the Town is laughing at the escapade of the Duke. The Wild young man exercised his shooting across Hanover Square and near killed poor old General Denbigh in the opposite house. They say the bullet whistled past his ear and lodged in the wainscotting. Ned returned utterly drunk last night from the Maccaroni Club. They are travelled Young Men who do great Execution with Spy glasses. He is very gay of late. Lost £15 at Whisk. 'Tis cards all day and night long, and 'tis Ill bred to refuse to play. I play like a Fool and am losing Heavily.

June 7th.

Miss D'Arcy sick. Pray heaven 'tis not the Smallpox. She will not permit me to visit her for fear it is, but I sent her flowers and also a Sweet embroidered purse to comfort her. Ned very unhappy to hear of her Indisposition.

Last night Ned and me went to an Assembly at Madame Cornelys at Carlisle House in Soho Square. Magnificent rooms and collation and a Crush that near killed me. Lord M——rd very attentive to me.

June 8th.

Miss D'Arcy recovered somewhat. Not the dread sickness. I spend all my Days now at Routs or at Mrs. Dantin,* Mount Street. Am growing thin.

* A fashionable Mantua maker of the day.—Ed.

June 10*th.*

Saw King and Queen out driving to-day. Not an Immoderately lovely couple, but I huzzahed and waved my handkerchief with the best of them. Burletta last evening at Convent Garden. Laughed till I near Split.

It seems there is a Plan on foot that Ned should be painted by Mr. Reynolds who is the Painter à la Mode now.* I declare I cannot see why Ned with his Carroty Locks should have his portrait made while my more worthy Features should go down unrecorded to the Tomb. Have prayed Papa to permit me to be painted by Miss Reid who is also very Modish but he declares he has not sufficient money for two, which I vow is a Monstrous shame.

June 11*th.*

Haymaking party. Amongst Guests : Lord M., Mr. Sutcliffe, Lord Tavistock and his pretty betrothed, Lady E. Keppell, Madame de Guerchey, Lady Mary Duncan and so on. Lord M——rd very attentive to

---

* This plan does not seem to have come to anything. There is no portrait of Ned Knox by Sir Joshua Reynolds on record.— Ed.

La Belle Irlandaise as he pleases to call me. Unluckily the weather broke and the rain spoiled our Sweet Bucolic Simplicity, soaking Pet Lambs, Muslin Frocks, and making us into a mob of drowned Rats.

June 13*th.*
Mr. Sutcliffe visits me nearly every morning at my toilette with books. Sits and glares like an idiot. Lost another £30 at Piquet the other day. My father's face will be grim when I inform him of this.

June 15*th.*
Lady H. is the greatest Rake in Town. Her minauderies are Intolerable.

June 16*th.*
Breakfast with Lady Temple. All the polite World present. Coffee, chocolate, biscuits, cream, buttered toasts, tea and Scandal. Mr. Sutcliffe took me to Bathoe in the Strand for Italian books. Pointed out to me Chevalier d'Eon, a strange looking Wretch. They tell the most curious tales of him. Some swear he is really a Female in disguise.

June 18*th.*

I spend half the day at the Hairdresser's now. My head has not been opened for over a Fortnight, and this is positively the longest time I will go in this hot weather, though some Ladies keep their Heads unopened till they are Intolerable to themselves and everyone else.   The dresser informed me that one lady from motives of thrift went so long a time that her head when opened was found to contain a Nest of Mice.   Lord save me from that ! We are to attend a grand Ball to-night at the Duchess of Queensbury.   She is a Whimsical clever woman.

June 19*th.*

Philosophical lecture with Mr. Sutcliffe. Somewhat wearisome.   Have hopes of seeing Lord M——rd at the Little Theatre to-night.

June 20*th.*

Was mightily distressed this morning. Out shopping perceived a Poor youth being conducted to execution for Highway robbery. He could not have been more than 18 with an Amiable, handsome countenance and an air of Breeding. What a Melancholy end for a foolhardy escapade. Mr. Sutcliffe thinks they hang for too Trifling Offences. If I was Queen of England I should change this, but most persons I talk to are all for Hanging everyone.

June 21*st.*

Attended a Magnificent Masque last night at Northumberland House, which did not cease till 7 in the morning.

I dressed as a Turkish slave in a rich costume of Silver cloth. 'Twas a Splendid sight. All the Beauties of the Town as Cleopatras, Goddesses, Shepherdesses and so on. One gentleman attired as a dead Corpse in a Shroud and carrying a Coffin. So Ghastly a spectacle that one lady swooned at the sight of him. Saw the famous, or some would say, infamous Miss Chudleigh in some sort of Undress. To my mind she is somewhat decayed. They say she is married to Mr. Hervey of the Navy. Supper and lighting on a grand scale. Ned declares there must have been no less than a 100 dishes. I believe he tasted of them all. One's head confused with it all. Duchess of

Rutland to my mind is marvellously handsome.

Lord M——rd prodigiously magnificent as a Turkish Sultan (could anything be more apropos ?). Danced many times with me and said glancing at my costume, " I must find a Sultana for myself, Ma'am," which Fluttered me a trifle. Wish I knew his meaning. Also complimented me on the length of my eye lashes.

June 23rd.

An odious and utterly Unexpected Mishap occurred to me last night ! Was returning with Lady D. from the play in her coach. 'Twas a dark raining night. As we passed through St. James' Square our horses stopped suddenly, there was a noise of scuffling and shouts, the window was pulled open, and a Masked Ruffian thrust his head in and presented a pistol at our breasts with the words, " Damee stand and deliver—off with those jewels now." Words cannot depict our Fright and Consternation. Lady D. in her anger swore like a Trooper and I very rashly attempted to jump out of the coach and call for the Watchman. A pistol held against my very bosom made me realise the hopeless position we were placed in. Weeping with Rage and Vexation I removed my Jewels, while Lady D. did likewise. The Villain then galloped away. I lay the night at Lady D.'s house being too agitated to return home and we spent half the night in Fruitless Lamentations. I have lost by this Dastardly Outrage the following ornaments—my diamond earrings left me by Great Aunt Caroline, my diamond and ruby chain and pendant given me by my dear Mama on her very death bed, a curious and antique pearl ring, two diamond rings, a bracelet set in brilliants and my jewelled fan. 'Tis Monstrous and Damnable that such a Thing should happen in London. Travelling in the country one may be prepared for Robbery, but Town should at all events be safe. The Watchmen are worse than useless. 'Tis Abominable. Lady D. and my father have offered large rewards to the Bow Street Runners, but they are Fools too and I dare swear we shall never see one of those trinkets again. Am too Vexed to go abroad to-day.

Have received many amiable messages from my friends condoling me.

June 25th.

Supper party last night given in my honour by Lord M. to console me, so he declared, for my recent highway robbery. A large Company present. All extremely Lively. Lord M. no eyes for anyone but me. He wrote my name on his wine glass with a diamond and then to my vast confusion pulled off my red satin slipper, filled it with wine, and drank my Health from it. This extravagance agitated me and seeing that most of the company were intoxicated, I pulled Ned to one side and made him escort me home.

This morning received a note from Lord M. as follows. " Lord M——rd's Compliments to Miss Knox. Hopes she was not Offended last night ? What was the reason for her sudden departure which robbed the Party of its Chief Grace ? He begs her to send him one of her Chemises, for he has vowed not to drink another drop of Wine that has not been strained through a Piece of her Underlinen."

This strange message somewhat Disconcerted me. For some time could not decide whether he was really madly Enamoured or merely insulting me. At length I decided that a bantering reply would be the most discreet under the circumstances, and I sent a line to the effect that Irish Lawn was too precious by far to be used as a Seive.

Miss D'Arcy to take tea to-day. She made me laugh heartily by showing to me a letter from a young Gentleman in the Army, who, being on Guard, responded to her invitation in this strange manner, " Captain Pole regrets he cannot accept Kind Invitation, but is Prematurely confined in the Tower" !

June 27th.

Ranelagh. Lord M——rd came up to me as meek as a Lamb and full of apologies. Wish to Heaven he would declare himself one way or another.

Very Gay Party with Lady T. She is the most Vivacious woman imaginable. Said to-day apropos of the new Gentry, " Lud ! I dare not spit out of the window now for fear of spitting on an Earl," which made us all scream. The story going the rounds is that the Duke of G. attempting to appease his mistress, Dolly Carsons, with whom he had had a Tiff, gave her a Bank Bill for £100, whereupon she cried, " Damn your money, what's the use of it," clapped it between two bits of Bread and eat it. I wish someone would offer it to me for I am in Debt to a Shocking Extent, and dare not inform Papa. I would borrow from Ned but he, it would seem, is still more Embarrassed. 'Tis all these Odious Cards that are to blame. I console myself by thinking that I could be in a Worse Case. I have seen a lady lose as much as £700 at a game.

June 30*th.*

Have been sick these last few days of l'influenza,* a Fashionable Sickness for many of my friends are suffering from it, but it has ended my Gaieties for a while.

My father ordered me to be bled, but I locked my door and lay abed silent though my father and the Surgeon battered on my door in a Fury. Thanks to Mrs. S.'s gruels

---

* It is surprising to find Miss Knox mentioning this fashionable modern illness under a slightly different form. Mrs. Montagu in her letters also talks of " l'influenza."—ED.

am now quite recovered though as weak as a Mouse.

July 2nd.

To-day taking the air in my chair, one of my Bearers fell in a hole in the road and all but threw me out onto the street. Saw the famous Gunning, Duchess of Hamilton, out. What a Fortune she and her sister* gained by their looks. No sign from Lord M. d——n him.

The town is growing Empty now.

July 3rd.

Went to a Drum † at Lady Waldgrave and heard all the Scandal I had missed by my Sickness. It seems that Lord P. wedded Lady E. H. chiefly to escape from 2 importunate mistresses. Another Droll tale is that poor Mr. Astor fell enamoured of Miss Johnson, daughter to a Poor country Squire, for her beautiful brown Locks. The morning after they were wed, lo and behold ! the slut threw her " tête " aside, displaying

---

* Lady Coventry. Supposed to have died from the effects of using too many cosmetics.—Ed.

† Drum was a name for a small party given by ladies.—Ed.

Carroty hair which colour Mr. Astor holds in particular Abhorrence.

Out to-day saw a Press gang seize upon 2 young men. Thought for a brief second there would be a Riot among the Mob to rescue them.

July 5th.

Guests including Mr. Sutcliffe to dinner at 3. Stayed till 8 exchanging Gossip and Compliments. Purchased some new caps and corsets for myself. Miss D'Arcy has given me an excellent Recipe for Lip Salve. Ned is abroad all night now with parties of wild blades, and seems to indulge in every kind of Rakery and Frolic from his account.

Last night, so it seems, at some tavern his friends threw the table and chairs out of window, and on the landlady remonstrating threw her after her chattels. Someone less drunk than the rest called out that she might be dead, whereupon some Tipsy Wit cried out, " Charge her in the bill." Happily for her and them the window was near the ground, and the poor woman was still alive and unhurt. I told Ned somewhat severely that these Excesses will lead him to Tyburn in a country where one is hanged for cutting down an Apple Tree. I added sharply that insulting women and knocking down feeble old watchmen was a poor kind of wit in my opinion, and upon this we had a Furious Quarrel which raged till my father ordered me to my room and Ned to leave the house.

July 6th.

Have made a most Astounding discovery to-day. Miss D'Arcy came to take tea with me and after sitting for some time in Deep Dejection suddenly broke out: " My dear friend, I must confide in you. I am in a most odious predicament. In short I am well—" enceinte." " What," I cried, " my Poor Child, have you been so foolish as to allow yourself to be . . ." " No, not at all," said she, a trifle offended and pulling out from her dress a Chain she is accustomed to wear round her neck, showed me a Wedding Ring attached to it. " Married," I cried, much relieved, " not that I would have set myself up to judge you for I as near as near did the other thing myself once." Anyhow, the whole story came out, how that she had made the acquaintance while visiting friends in Shropshire, of a young naval officer of Poor but Genteel parentage. They had become mutually Enamoured, and knowing that her Parents would never permit them to wed, they had the ceremony performed in secrecy.

He is on service now and she, poor Lady, in the condition she confessed to me. We sat for over 3 hours discussing her Predicament, but after consuming a vast quantity of Tea and Cakes were still monstrously undecided. At length I counselled her to confess the whole affair to her parents, or if her Courage failed her, I myself was willing to break the news to them.

She departed somewhat Fortified, and is to inform me to-morrow of her Decision.

Who would ever have suspected such a thing? I own I Quail somewhat at the prospect of informing Mr. D'Arcy of his Daughter's Indiscretion. I tremble to think of Ned's vexation when he hears of it, for I truly believe he is catched by her.

July 7th.

* Here I am locked up in my chamber,

* Miss Knox's handwriting at this entry was almost unreadable.—Ed.

my eyes so swollen with crying that I can scarcely see out of them. I believe to day has been the most Terrible of my life. Misfortunes appear to be overwhelming me. Early this morning I received a distracted letter from poor Delia D'Arcy bidding me an Eternal Farewell. She has confessed all, and her parents are dispatching her away post haste to an Aunt, Lady Montgomery, in the wilds of Devonshire to repent at leisure. I wept somewhat at perusing this and wondered if I should ever set eyes on my poor Friend again. Then to add to my misery, that fool Mr. Sutcliffe, took it into his Head to wait on my father and ask for my Hand. My father summoned me to the parlour when he had left, and informed me of his offer adding that he hoped I would accept it, as Mr. Sutcliffe was an " excellent young man "; these were his very words, and the owner of a good property in Sussex. I regret to say that I flew into a Pretty Passion at this, declaring that I would as soon wed a Mute as that long-visaged, melancholy Idiot and that I wished to Heaven my father would leave me in Peace. While we were wrangling in this manner, he roaring at me and I commencing to Weep, in came Ned and had the Impudence to give his opinion on the matter, saying that I was a Damned fool not to take a good offer like that, and still more of a Fool to hang around hoping for that Rake Lord M———rd to declare himself! This remark provoked me so terribly that I turned on him exclaiming: " Well, sir, let me tell you that Miss D'Arcy is a married Woman "; whereupon Ned's curses were so terrible that I was forced to clap my hands over my ears.

My father in a fury drove us out of the room, and me up to my chamber. Later he came to me, and declared that I had grown alarmingly Passionate and Ill humoured of late since my stay in Town, and he could not think what had come over me.

" Now girl," he said, " have some sense and take Mr. S."

At this I stamped my foot and said: " I will never wed anyone but Mr. Ancaster, and these are my last words on the subject."

" Very well," roared my father, " very well. You shall stay up here till your temper has abated," and slammed the door to, adding as he went out, " What you require, Miss, is a good bleeding."

'Tis true enough I have been in a Vile Mood this last week or so. I believe it is the Heat. Heaven, or rather my father, knows how long I shall be confined up here.*

July 8th.

Nothing to write for I am still cruelly confined to this room. The servants dare not release me, for Papa is as Absolute as the King of France.†

July 9th.

A fresh calamity has occurred. Ned contrived to slip into my room looking very flustered, when the Footman brought me my dinner. Fell upon me with the words: " My dear Cleone, I am in a damnable scrape." In short, Ned, like the Idiot he is, has picked a quarrel with a Young Gentleman of Importance (no less a person than a cousin of Mr. Pitt's) who has challenged him

* The Editor has here deleted a page of love-lorn raptures about Mr. Ancaster.

† A current expression of the time alluding to Louis XV.'s absolute power.—ED.

to a Duel. I am, by some means or other to induce my father to depart prematurely for Bath, while Ned remains behind on pretence of staying with Mr. Richards at his villa at Knightsbridge. Gracious Heaven, this is an odious business! If he slays his opponent I should not be astonished if he was obliged to fly the country.* I cannot think why these hateful calamities have occurred all in a Heap. No more now.

* This fear of Miss Knox, which at first sight seems curious at a time when duelling was so common, was in part justified. Duelling in the 18th century was a criminal offence in the eyes of the law and in some cases punishable by hanging.—ED.

IV

BATH

IV

BATH

July 12th.

I write this at Woolhampton at the Rising Sun Inn.   A moderately easy journey. Passed securely through Hounslow Heath and Maidenhead Thicket unmolested by Road Inspectors.*   Most unhappily however poor Paddy has utterly disgraced himself, and my father has been constrained to dismiss from our service this Faithful and hitherto Trusty Retainer.   A most unlooked for Misfortune.   Occurred in this manner. To-day, a little way past Reading, the Stage Coach came up at a Swift Pace and outstripped our Chariot, the coachman meanwhile jeering at our domestics.   Paddy, mortified, whipped on the horses, the Stage quickened up and so we raced neck to neck, careering round corners at a terrible Pace and rocking from Side to Side.   Papa cursed, the passengers screamed, Mrs. S. and self were Thrown violently in a Heap. Thank the Lord our hind wheel stuck in a

---

* A slang term for highwaymen.—Ed.

rut, and only this I am convinced, saved us from overturning. The Stage speedily out-distanced us. Papa, mad with Rage, damned Paddy in a Frightful Manner. The poor Wretch unable to give any reason for this Wicked Mad conduct but, maintained with tears in his eyes his passionate desire to Vindicate the Family Honour in the eyes of the Stage. Am sure 'twas nothing but an unpremeditated Impulse on the part of the poor Rash Wretch, but Papa declares we could never trust him now on the Continent. This Inn is more like a country residence, for Lord S——n is lying here, and has in his customary domineering fashion made the place His Own even to putting the Domestics in his livery.

July 13*th*.

This place is filled with gouty old noble-men and their ladies, statesmen, poets, writers, admirals, beauties, Beaux and fortune hunters. All meet in the Pump Room, drink water and exchange Gossip. Thankful I have my elegant Town Wardrobe. Do not know if I shall care for this place, but am vastly happy to be away from Town, where

my last days were rendered Odious by Papa,
the heat and Lord M.   My father treats me
with great solicitude, the result of my fit of
Vapours in Town, but Lud ! I tremble to
think of his wrath if he could but know what
Ned was up to ! I shall not be easy in my
mind till this hateful Rencontre is safely
finished with.   Though Ned has often
Plagued me in the Past, I pray Highest
Heaven he will not be run through.   My
father escorted me to the chief physician here,
and remained closeted with him some time,
doubtless demanding him what Malady is the
cause of my Infatuation for Mr. A. and my
recent Wilfulness.   At all events, the pompous Medico after examining my tongue and
gazing down my throat, prescribed for me a
course of Medicinal waters adding: " Res
est soliciti plena timori amor.   Vitiant artus
————* contagia mentis."   To which my
father replied: " Varium et mutabile semper
Faemina."   And they both laughed to my
vexation.   Papa informs me that this Latin
stands for: " Love is the perpetual source of

* Miss Knox has omitted this word, which is obviously
intended to be " aegrae."—Ed.

fear and anxiety. When the mind is ill at ease, the body is in a certain degree affected," and also: " Woman is always changeable and capricious," which shows plainly what fools men are.

July 14*th.*

This is a beautiful place, set in an amphitheatre of rocky and wooded hills, and has spacious and elegant houses and a fine Abbey Church, but for my part I am already a trifle weary of it, though heaven knows 'tis crowded enough with the Beau Monde. I have met several of my London acquaintances, but 'tis nothing but Complaints of Vapours and Gout, Stale Scandal dished up from the past season and spiteful cries of, " Heavens, look at her face." " Lud ! how plain she is grown," and so on. No news from Ned.

July 15*th.*

To church. A sermon so lengthy that I near died. Dozed behind my fan.

July 16*th.*

To the Baths for the first and last time, that's flat ! Clad in a Bonnet, Jacket and

Petticoat (a costume that does not become me) the Ladies here contrive to conduct watery flirtations and Intrigues as happily as on Terra Firma. Each lady is provided with a little Tray ladened with sweetmeats and perfumes, and when these float away out of reach the gentlemen swim after them gallantly, to the Admiration of the Spectators in the gallery.

Miss Ralston in particular was as Frolicsome as a Mermaid and displayed a very fine pair of arms. For my part I feel too Healthy now I am out of Town, to enjoy being conveyed in a chair swathed in blankets as if I was a gouty old Dame, and I have no "beau" with whom to disport myself in the water. Apropos of these Baths, Miss R. tells me a diverting little "conte", how that last season a Dowager Marchioness of excessively Tall stature and overweening pride ordered the Bath to be filled to her chin, whereupon all the Ladies of lower rank and height were obliged to hasten out or be drowned !

July 17*th.*

Time passes here in the same insipid, gay

manner every day. Morning in Undress at private or public breakfasts, drinking waters, baths ; evening prayers at the Abbey for the Devout, social parades, visits to the Libraries and book-sellers, the Eternal Cards. After dinner more parades, tea, drives and perhaps a Ball at the Assembly Rooms. I wish Ned were here, for he would Enjoy the Cricket which all the young gentlemen here indulge in. Old gentlemen abound here, and are never Weary of informing one how marvellously Refined and Decorous the Society was in the Golden Days of Beau Nash, " before, ma'am, all these Damned tradesmen and negro drivers made it all so common." The young gentlemen write verses, little tortured vers d'esprits to their Belles, and they are entered in a book at the booksellers. I have had 3 addressed to me, but they are Too Insipid and Weak to waste time and Paper upon copying them in. I suspect that they find my name not an easy one for rhyming, else one poor Youth would not have been constrained to couple Cleone with *Moaning!*

July 18*th.*

Lord G.——* has arrived here with a Blackamoor and 3 kept mistresses in his retinue. What Lady G. thinks of this Seraglio is not reported. She retires to the Wells for her Bathing and doubtless consoles herself. Apropos of Negros, I saw the following notice in the newspaper here: " Black Boy for sale, Docile and obedient. Answers to the name of Toby," which so catched me that I wished to answer it, but my father sternly forbid me to add to our Retinue which already it seems, is costly enough. He makes great Complaints of our expenditure in Town and forbids me to purchase any more Wardrobe for some little time. I walk here everyday in the Meadows and by the River Avon. Papa and I ride together.

July 19*th.*

Am vexed to-day. No sound from Ned. Heaven help the poor Foolish Youth. Also Miss R. in conversation on various people mentioned Lord M——rd, and declared that

---

* Miss Knox has an annoying habit, common to her age, of mentioning people of exalted position by initials only when she is relating some piece of scandal about them.—Ed.

he was Loved by half the women of Fashion in Town, but that he would never be dragged to the Altar by anyone of them in her opinion, for he had several mistresses, and though many beautiful young Ladies had striven to capture him, some even being Complaisant beyond the bounds of Virtue and Prudence in an attempt to compromise him, he had each time eluded their grasp. It seems that when they weep and lay the blame for their ruin on him, he replies with the utmost callousness: "Dear Madam, why distress yourself? There is always the Foundling Hospital." I think now with Deep Mortification of certain Vain Foolish hopes which I once cherished. Is it likely that a man who can have half the Beauties of London as his concubines would deign to offer poor me the coveted Title of Sultana?

I shall pluck his now Hateful image from my heart, thankful that though humiliated I have at all events preserved my Good Name.

July 20*th.*

Fulfilled my promise to Mrs. Soames and examined Mrs. Winters' Seminary for Young Ladies here. I do not believe Elizabeth

Soames would thrive in such a place. Mrs. W. makes a monstrous to do about her instruction which if one is to believe her, comprises Latin, Greek, Hebrew, French, Italian, Dancing, Music, Keeping Accompts, Arithmetic, Singing, History, Pastry Cooking, Lud ! I have forgot what else, but I observed that the Pupils were Dirty and Ill kempt, and I doubt if they are taught Grace of Carriage by their general Deportment. I should not be astonished also if they were kept short of Food.

A new married couple, Mr. and Mrs. Chetwyn, arrived here on their Wedding trip accompanied by Mrs. Peel their Aunt. They are excessively young, 17 and 18 respectively, and were wedded by Force to cancel a Gambling Debt between their Parents, but seem vastly happy notwithstanding.

July 21*st*.

A play acted in a Barn near here by the fashionable youth of the place, in which I played the role of "Clarissa", a young country lady who is betrayed by a noble Rake. Thankful that though the Bucolic character of the part fits me, the other does not through some Happy Chance, for I own to my shame that I have not always shewn sufficient prudence, especially where Mr. David Ancaster was concerned ; so Fatal an effect does swarthy masculine beauty produce upon my too susceptible Heart.

The play was poorly acted as might have been anticipated from the rehearsals, where all the players wrangled and complained of their Roles. " My dear, I vow I cannot be an Ingenue ! 'Tis too Insipid ! Let me be the fascinating Lady Georgina ! I am immoderately skilful at passionate scenes," and so on. My Noble Rake, far from being the Bold Villain he was pictured in the play, was seized all on a sudden with a fit of fright and totally forgot his words till I pinched his arm sharply, whereupon he bleated: " Clarissa, I am determined to have you Body and Soul" in a voice like a sheep ! Before 'twas ended it commenced to rain and the Barn being Old and Decayed, the spectators retired home damp and melancholy.

July 23rd.

Ned arrived by post chaise, excessively

pallid, arm in sling. Mr. P. wounded in Lungs and is hovering between life and death. Decided after consultation that the sooner we reach France the better, lest the worst should happen. Juries, owing to Mr. P.'s Influential position would in all certainty pass a severe verdict. Pray Heaven we can persuade my father to move. No more now, for there is much to be done. To convey at such short notice an Obstinate Father, family coach, 5 domestics and impedimenta is no easy Task. Papa at my Ernest intercession has pardoned Paddy, but Mrs. S. to my vast amazement, has utterly refused to brave yet another sea voyage, which is damnably odious of her. She is to remain here with Lady Brownlow and I shall hire a Frenchwoman to take her part. Papa very Vexed at this.

V

FRANCE

V

FRANCE

July 28th.—Amiens.

My father's ill opinion of the French fully
confirmed, for on arriving here, we discovered
that the Innkeeper at Calais had pilfered our
boxes and stolen a quantity of linen ruffles
and a gilt snuff box. On the other hand
'tis not Impossible that they were purloined
on board the Pacquet Boat, for we were all
as uneasy as anything after 8 hours passage,
and not caring for anything except to be set
on shore once more.

Ned and me much Diverted to find ourselves in this strange Country, and I hung
my head out of the coach window all the
journey down to this place admiring the
sights, but my father complains greatly of
the rain which he never observes in his
native land, but which vexes him here; the
French louis for which he reluctantly parts
with his precious Sterling, and the Rapacity
of the people in general.

A great quantity of English pass this route,
and we are expected to path our way with

gold. Ned had a sharp Dispute with the Customs apropos of a new Green Plush coat. He speaks the language admirably, to my astonishment.

The country round here is poor and but indifferently pretty, but the roads are superb. Inns bad, with poor wine and bread, but I am delighted at the newness of it all, the Poplars, clothes of French peasants, unaccustomed Tongue, and we have occasional glimpses of fine Chateaux. I am vain enough to be Diverted with the Attention and Curiosity our appearance excites. This Town seems prosperous. A cavalry regiment quartered here. Two very genteel young officers escorted us around the Gothic Cathedral which we visited to-day, explaining all the Beauties of it to us. Was gratified to note that I can converse very Tolerably in French. Believe I shall be happy in this Country; if Mr. A. were but here.

July 29th.

Travellers see Curious sights indeed. Last evening 2 young gentlemen arrived at our Auberge in a chaise. Both elegantly attired, one smaller and younger than the other.

To all appearances Brothers. I observed that the younger brother seemed vexed when the tall young man cast a casual sheep's eye in my direction, but thought no more of it. This morning coming downstairs I passed their chamber and glanced in, the door being ajar. What was my surprise to perceive seated on the bed in Deshabille not 2 young men, but One young man and a Pretty girl with long black hair. Yet two young Gentlemen left the Inn half an hour later.

Indeed, this is a strange country where such Miracles occur! Who the young Friends were no one can tell me, nor is it my business to know, but it has given me an idea for my next Masquerade. I vow I should look monstrous fine in Breeches and a Tie Wig.

*August 6th.—Chanteloup.**

Never have I seen or indeed dreamed of any place so magnificent as this. 'Tis truly more a palace than a mere dwelling place. The rooms are large, spacious, and furnished in the heights of Elegance and Taste, many hung with exquisite Tapestry. My own

* The Knox's do not seem to have stopped at Paris. They evidently went straight on to Chanteloup.—Ed.

room is the prettiest I have seen for some time, with a charming gilded bed hung with Rose satin, Toilette tables and chairs en suite. The walls are hung with rare tapestry depicting the Life of Venus. Everywhere one glances are fine gilt mirrors, clocks and vases of priceless value. 'Tis fit for a Princess, for every article in the room is an objet de luxe. Down below all equally fine. The style is excessively Formal, but in keeping, in my opinion, with the place. Attached to the house is an Immense Pleasure ground which I have not yet had leisure to observe carefully, but it supplies this Mansion with a Thicket of sweet scented and rare Flowers and Fruit. Have been so utterly bewildered by all the Sumptuousness that I have not dared approach my journal. My poor pen is not equal to the Task of describing it. The Duchesse * treats us with the greatest Amiability and shows us every Egards. She is Charming and Petite. The weather has become so Excessively Hot that we are mightily thankful to reserve our stay in Paris

* Duchesse de Choiseul, wife of Duc de Choiseul, Minister of Louis XV.—ED.

till later. The guests here are numerous, everything being on a gigantic scale, and I have not yet been able to ascertain their names and titles as yet, but all belong to the Haute Noblesse. Among others the Duc de Nivesnoir, Duchesse de Cosse and Duchesse de La Valliere who is excessively handsome, though over 50 years of age. The Va et Vient however is Prodigious and new Guests arrive every Hour. A great Bustle and Buz if ever there was one. The Ladies here wear Immense Heels. Their Heads smaller than in England, but excessively Fuzzed. They are Witty and Elegant, but do not possess to my mind the fine forms and complexions of Englishwomen. Indeed 'tis hard to say what kind of faces they have, for they are all Rouged and Painted to an Immoderate degree. What they think of my Appearance and Hair 'tis hard to say. I believe they consider my foreign dress and speech piquant, at all events they treat me with great courtesy. One lady informed me indeed that the french prefer the Irish to the English, who according to her account **have** Uncouth Manners when travelling on the Continent, and will even

appear in genteel french society in Hunting
Suits, which causes Vast Scandal. I am
Vastly Surprised at the Tone in general of
the Conversation which is utterly different
from what I had thought 'twould be. Had
expected Frivolity, but the talk here among
both sexes is of nothing but Politics, Literature and Religion. I own I am somewhat
melancholy at finding this Grave Air. The
Gentlemen are stiff and Philosophical. The
Ladies are all Savante or pretend to be. I am
not prepared to swear that they do not indulge
in Affairs de Coeur, and that the men are not
Fond and the ladies frail like plain mortals,
but at all events they have a very curious
manner of conducting their Intrigues. I
think Mr. A. would be very Melancholy here.

For the rest our mode of life is sumptuous
and we pass our days in Elegant Leisure.
The morning as we please. Dinner at 3
or 15 o'clock as 'tis called quaintly in France.
Cards and conversation with our Hostess,
bed when we choose, in short, all Very
dégagé except for Supper when we dress as
Magnificently as if at Versaille. No De-
mands of " When are you going ? " or " Why

don't you do this or t'other?" We live like Gods and Goddesses upon Olympia. The domestics comprise a small Army. Ned declares there must be no less than 400, indoor and outside. My father lost in admiration of the Pigeries and Poultry Yards.

August 7th.

A letter from my dear Cary. It seems that William is the lustiest Babe for his age, that ever was seen in Derbyshire. Sir C. Mills is to wed a Widow.

August 10th.

A play acted most admirably in the private theatre here. Even the performances of the most noted English actors would seem Insipid to me besides this Vivacious and Witty Miming. Their very hands seemed to speak. I own I find the french more entertaining on than off the stage. The talk now is of nothing but Religion or rather Abuse of it. 'Tis the Mode to be an Atheist and a Heathen. Monsieur de Belisle a relative and protégé of the Duchess, expressed Prodigious Contempt when I confessed that I was a Devout Protestant. "Fancy, Mademoiselle is a dévote " he announced sneeringly to the Company and there was a general titter. I was Revenged notwithstanding this, for later he mentioned Richardson's " Clarissa Harlowe " in terms of highest praise, whereupon 'twas for me to cry out that the Novelist was utterly Demodé now in England. The young man in Question is short and has no chin and besides, all this Philosophy in my opinion does not add to the attraction of a young gentleman. How different indeed from my ardent Mr. A. Pray Heaven I shall find a letter from him in Paris. My father declares that he observes a vast alteration in french manners since he visited this country as a young man. Then, the Petits Maitres talked and thought of nothing but Gallantry. He is prepared to wager that these Intellectual Airs are but a superficial covering for the National Licentiousness.

August 11*th.*

Out riding to-day in the forest with a party of ladies and gentlemen. Monsieur de Belisle, perhaps thinking that my figure looked well in a riding suit, attached himself to me and attempted to convert me to Atheism.

But I laughed in his face and rode ahead so fast that he could not keep up with me. My horsemanship much praised to Papa by the company. The forest here is magnificent with broad roads cut in it. It is well stocked with deer and boars. Returning home by the high road we passed by a village. Was astonished by the dirtiness and general aspect of poverty. The cottages were hovels, peasants unkempt and some barely clothed. More like parts of Ireland, but my father declared he would be ashamed to see *his* tenants in Co. Down in such a filthy and disorderly state. It seems that the taxes are very heavy on the " tiers états," the nobles and clergy are free from this, which doubtless accounts for their great riches. I have a coverlid on my bed composed entirely of Venice point, my sheets trimmed with the finest lace. Thank Heaven, I have a lovely wrapper and cap of rose satin, or I should not dare to lie in all this splendour.

August 12*th.*

Some of the company here are excessively strange. Madame d'Harcourt who is lovely to a degree, is affectation itself. She never blows her nose for fear of spoiling its outline, but dabs at it with a piece of lawn which her page carries for her. She refuses also to eat anything in public except fruit and biscuits. This morning she informed me she cannot sleep except in a sitting position with flowers on her pillow, and other absurdities. She has had three husbands, all of whom she has driven to their graves, and heaven knows how many lovers, although she is not more than thirty five or so. Madame la Comtesse de Brinoy de Chateauroux on the other hand is a most elegant and charming lady. She must be more than sixty years, yet she has all the vivacity and fascination of a young woman. Her form is slim and supple, her skin soft and fresh as a child's. She possesses in short an elegant mind and body. She treats me with great amiability, and has given me some Valuable Advice with regard to Mr. A. and Men in General. This morning in the enclosed garden where I helped her gather herbs to make into a complexion wash she said " My dear Child, do you know how I have Retained my looks ? All my life I have been loved and all my life I have eaten vegetables. Do the same and if you do not use too much rouge, you will keep your youth beyond the usual limit ; in short, you will have a longer lease of life than the rest of your sex, for to be ugly is to be as good as dead." All this is very true.

August 13*th.*

Last night our hosts held a fête champêtre. A magnificent affair. The grounds all illuminated with torches and lanterns. A sumptuous supper served in the hall and in the garden. Sprightly music, and a troupe of Opera Dancers performing on the lawn. There was even a flock of lambs festooned with blue ribbons to give a bucolic air. The guests were all attired as Shepherds and Shepherdesses or Greek Gods and so on. Madame de Brinoy had the goodness to assist me with my costume. As Pomona, Nymph of Gardens, I wore a green gown ornamented with flowers, grapes in my hair and a silver pruning knife in one hand. Looked very passable indeed. A party of gypsies hired by the Duchesse to tell fortunes in the Rose Garden. One swarthy hag seized my hand and poured out a stream of prophecy. Among a great deal of foolishness one remark of hers seems to me worthy of note. She declared that my fate was a handsome dark young man who loved me passionately, that there were difficulties in our path, but that if I wished for happiness, I must remain faithful to him. This without any doubt points most clearly to Mr. A. She then declared that Happiness would come to me on the water, and incomprehensible though this is to me, I heartily pray it may be true.

Happened during the Fête to observe an incident which caused me some surprise. Was near the wood to look for a fan I had dropped, when a Bacchante ran lightly across the grass. She looked round and made a sign. Whereupon she was joined by a gentleman dressed as a Satyr and they hurried hand in hand into the thicket. I meanwhile being hidded in the shadow of a tree, perceived by the light of the moon that the couple were Madame d'Harcourt and Monsieur de Damville.

Turning to go I perceived at my elbow no less a person than Madame de Damville—

a captivating blonde. She was smiling very quizzingly behind her mask and pointing in their direction with her fan, she observed in the coolest way imaginable. " La-la Mademoiselle, my husband and la belle Madame d'Harcourt have gone away to philosophise together—doubtless— " then seeing my astonishment she said " Don't look so pained child. Are there no unfaithful husbands in your country ? " With that she strolled away.

Though I am no prude, I own that I am mighty surprised at such Cynical Complaisance on the part of an injured Wife, and somewhat disgusted at the Hypocrisy of these French in general.

August 16*th*.

The weather so oppressive these last few days that no one has the strength to do more than stroll in the gardens, Philosophical conversation is at a standstill, the heat having exhausted what wits we have. I have hardly the courage to attend to my Journal, though to-day it is by far the best company in the place. 'Tis mightily hard to be good-humoured in this weather. This morning

Madame d'Harcourt threw a plate at her page. My Father and Comte de Coligny had a heated discussion apropos of the British Crown Jewels which Monsieur de C. declares are mere replicas dating from King George I., the originals having been stolen by the Stuarts. My Father though in truth no very staunch Hanoverian, considered this a slight on the national honour and all but gave Monsieur de C. the lie direct. Ned, whom I have scarcely exchanged a word with all the visit, declares he is near dead of ennui. The ladies here, in his opinion, are all head and no heart. He supposes that they can be wooed like other females, but swears he cannot please them. Little Madame de Sechelles de Vautrin seems indeed to have showed him some signs of favour, but to his vexation turns off his compliments with epigrams which he neither understands or wishes to. Monsieur de Belisle is very genteel and polite to me, and expressed a hope that we should meet in Paris. Madame de Brinoy, on my informing her of this, warned me against the man, though why she should do so I cannot conceive, for he has shown me nothing but the merest politeness.

August 17*th.*

Riding party in forest. Dinner served on ground. In evening " Phèdre " acted in theatre. Very wearisome in my opinion, but did not dare say so except to Mme. de B. who heartily agreed.

August 19*th.*

Madame de B. is the most excellent company possible. She has told me all manner of witty tales about the Court and people of her acquaintance. In her opinion the late Mme. de Pompadour was not such a marvellous beauty, though she had a certain brilliance in her youth. Indeed, she cannot think by what fascination she gained such a continued power over the King. Mme. de B., when she saw her a few years ago, says she was pale and delicate with blue eyes and a sickly complexion, and no eyebrows or eyelashes to speak of; and this last we agreed is a hideous defect in a woman. Madame de B. herself is blonde, but possesses pretty fair brows and grey eyes full of sprightly

Laughter. Madame de P. also it seems had false teeth and an awkward manner. Madame de B. declares that a certain style of Ugliness in a wicked woman is pleasing to the opposite Sex, which seems a very wrong thing indeed. It seems that everyone is wondering who will fill the post of Maîtresse en Titre left vacant by the decease of Madame de Pompadour. Madame de Brinoy who combines Liveliness with Good Sense, thinks it highly ill that France should be governed in this manner by dissolute women. " The People," she informed me to-day with a Grave air " are starving. What can they think when they observe the Folly and the Luxury of the Noblesse."

In the evening here the guests sing or recite for the entertainment of the others, and I observe that the french perform in public without a trace of Shyness. The Duchesse begged me to sing, so I gave the company an Irish ballad on the Battle of the Boyne, and then a little shepherd song in their own Language commencing " Maman, dites moi ce qu'on sent quand on aime." Was much applauded and all exclaimed on the feeling

I threw into the words. Indeed, my thoughts were with dear D. A. all the time I sang. Madame de B. is instructing me in another little bergerette entitled " Ah que ma voix me devient chère Depuis que mon berger se plaît à l'écouter," which she informs me was a great favorite of the Defunct Pompadour.

August 23rd.

Among the guests here is a young Abbé of 17, who must truly be the most Lively Cleric in the world. He is a Beau Garçon, rides, sings, dances and makes Love to perfection. In short takes his spiritual duties very easily. Also an old Marquis de Dunfort who keeps the Company in shrieks of merriment Malgré Lui. He is as ancient as Noah but thinks himself a very great Beau and Lady Killer indeed. He attires himself sumptuously but in the mode of Louis Quatorze, viz: great red heels, huge scented wig, amber cane like a Maypole and ribbons. He will discourse for hours if permitted upon his Antique Gallantries, and carries a portrait of Madame de Montespan in his Snuff box. The young Abbé (who by the way is said

to be the Fils par Aventure of a very Grand
Personage indeed) asked him jestingly if he
had ever been au mieux with Gabrielle
d'Estrées, which made him very vexed! He
declares that Ladies nowadays, dress, speak,
and make Love like Servant Girls. This old
Monster, strangely enough, possesses a young
and lovely wife. This morning he insisted
upon taking the air with me, and so we
strolled in the garden, he pretending to give
me his arm with gallantry but in reality
leaning heavily upon me. We had paused
for a second to admire a statue of Eros, and
he was entrain of informing me what a Mad
Success he was with the fair Sex, when we
overheard his lady from a bower saying in a
clear shrill voice, " Ah, chère Madame la
Duchesse, les vieux Maris, le mieux qu'ils
ont à faire c'est de s'en aller " at which I near
split with laughter.

August 28*th.*

The days pass here in such an Agreeable
and yet Trivial manner that I have found
nothing to record of late in this book.

Among the recent guests are Madame la
Marquise de Montfleux and her daughter,

who is but 15 and a captivating Blonde cendrée. The latter very agreeable to me. She has but this moment left her Convent and is to wed soon a wealthy Widower of 50, whom she has never even set eyes upon. To my amazement she contemplates this Frightful Fate with Tranquility. The mariage de convenance here is the general custom. If I had been a frenchwoman Papa would have wedded me to Mr. Sutcliffe in a twinkling of an Eye, so thank Heaven who saw fit to have me born in Co. Down. Madame d'Harcourt came down this evening her head covered with gold powder. A monstrous spectacle, for she is a brunette and nothing could become her more ill.

September 1st.—Near to Chateaudun.

Nothing could be more Filthy than this Inn. The Food indeed is excellent but the furniture is scanty, and the windows and doors will not close unless Marie Bonheur * and self put all our weight against them. Indeed, I wish I was in my sumptuous bed at Chanteloup. Parted yesterday from our kind hosts with many Compliments and Thanks.

* Marie Bonheur was her new maid.—Ed.

Madame de Brinoy on parting presented me
with a pair of captivating hyacinth * earings
and I am to wait upon her at her hotel in
Town.   To add to my discomfort the room
next to me is occupied by a Dead Corpse.
The landlady's son died yesterday and Marie
Bonheur, on entering the Chamber of Death
broke into Fearful Screams.   Papa says
women are Damned Fools and how can a
Dead body harm me, but I wish to Heaven
'twas not so plaguey near.

September 2nd.—Chartres.

Thankful to have arrived at length at this
fine Cathedral Town for we have had a
cruelly Unpleasant journey.   Last night we
were caught in a Thunder Storm, the rain
fell in torrents with most alarming flashes of
Lightening.   Our wheels stuck fast in the
muddy ruts.   In short, we were glad to ask
for shelter at a Farm House, for we were
far from any inn or town.   The owner of the
farm was mightily surprised at seeing persons
of our Quality and Nationality on his doorstep at that time of night, but his wife hastened

---

* Hyacinth was an old word for jacinth.—Ed.

forward and declared that she would be over-joyed to give us Hospitality. Exhausted as I was, I could not help observing the Poverty and Squalor of the whole place, for the kitchen, though moderately large, was almost devoid of Furniture, no glass in the windows, rain leaking through the Roof and so on. So utterly different from the Prosperous dwellings of my Papa's tenants in Co. Down, which are almost without fail Warm and Clean, with a Ham or so hanging from the Rafters. The children too, a small army of whom swarmed over the floor, were dirty and barefooted. Marie Bonheur in great high Feather informed our good Hostess from what I could overhear, that we were English Princes of high rank and so we were treated with great Egards. Rickety chairs were brought forward, children were hurried out of the way. The son of the house pro-duced a Hare and offered to let us eat it for our supper, praying us to say nothing about it, and making a great to do. Ned and my father at length discovered that he had shot it on his lord's capitanerie, and for this Trivial Poaching crime could be sent to the

Gallies if he were discovered. Papa not only promised silence but gave him a Louis in exchange, which sent him into Raptures. The Seigneur appears to have power of life and death in this land. Our host's pretty daughter had an infant at her side more decently attired than the others which she displayed to me with some pride, but I could not comprehend her Patois. Marie Bonheur explained to me later that this Infant is the result of Droit de Seigneur, a Curious privilege of the nobility which modesty prevents me describing more fully. Spent night on a hard bed. Ned and Papa in chairs. The Family, I imagine, on the floor or in cupboards. Set off this morning in the fashion of a Triumphal Procession. The peasants generously rewarded for our night's rest. The children ran after our coach for sous, which I threw them out of the window. To-day being the Sabbath, the population here are all hastening to Mass. My father desired to read some sermons to Ned and me, there being no Protestant church here, but when the time came Ned was found to be gone, no one knew where.

September 6th.—Paris.

My father has secured the services of Madame Dupont, an excellent, good-humoured female, to be my Companion. Madame la Duchesse recommended her as she is the Widow of her nephew's tutor, so I believe she will fill the Faithless Mrs. Stewart's place very tolerably. Paris very empty as yet, but I am glad of this, for 'twill give me leisure to observe it before I am plunged in a social Bustle, also to replenish and titivate my Wardrobe. Marie Bonheur, like all Parisians, has admirable taste and will advise me on the matter of caps, hoops which are worn here in moderation, and perfumes. I do not wish to proclaim my Insular nationality too plainly by my general appearance.

No letter from Mr. A. though I will own I had fully trusted to find one from him at M. Lafayette the Banker. This is excessively Vexatious. Surely he cannot be already Weary of me. I am apprehensive lest my last letter was in some way or other foolish, too complaisant or perhaps not affectionate enough to please him. Lud ! How these villainous men are Capricious.

September 8th.

We are very well pleased with this house which is situated in the Faubourg St. Honoré and is commodious with a fair sized garden, Spacious rooms and long windows. Fine furnishings and Mirrors enough to satisfy a Narcissus. On the other hand, 'tis not over clean and would doubtless be hateful in the cold season, but this must be borne with.

September 11th.

Waited on Lady Hertford the wife of our Ambassador here, who received us with the greatest Courtesy. She has promised to present me to their Majesties and puts herself entirely at our Service. The streets of this town are Vile and Dirty after London, and monstrously narrow for the crowd of noblemens coaches and chairs that throng them. Some even in the good quarters of the city are divided by gutters, and so after a day of rain are like swollen torrents. The houses are nothing but wood and plaster, and crumbling to bits at that. The Palais de Justice and Opera House fine, but most of the town stinks vilely, though to hear the french talk you would think 'twas Paradise

itself.   The poor people here attire themselves
in Black and Lady H. says 'tis on account of
the mud splashed up by the coaches.

September 14*th.*

To-day was presented to their Majesties,
the King and Queen at Versaille. My Lady
Hertford and Madame de Rochfort, my
sponsors for the ceremony.   I attired myself
in white Satin and wore my Diamonds, yet
was not utterly satisfied with my looks, for
I have grown thin of late.   Ned so resplendent
in Crimson brocade that I could not refrain
from whispering to him as we entered the
Royal apartments: " I vow you should be
announced as the Duke of Portaferry, my
dear Ned," which vexed the poor lad. The
ceremony of Presentation was as follows:
We were named to the King by the first
gentleman in waiting, my name being sent
in first. His Majesty kissed me on one cheek,
and then after a second's hesitation saluted
the other, but did not utter a word. My
father and Ned then presented, and I passed
on with the ladies to the Queen, where I made
a Deep Reverence.   Was then hastened on

to the Dauphin and Dauphiness,* Mesdames of France † and the young Duc de Berry,‡ Comtes de Provence § and Artois ‖ till I vow I was sick to death of them all. Lady H. says the King showed me great favour in saluting both cheeks, for this he usually does only to Grandees, women of Quality receiving the single Kiss alone. Notwithstanding, I would gladly exchange this Royal Kiss for a Wink from the faithless Mr. A.

As to the appearance of the Royal Family 'tis easy described. Louis the Well Beloved is Handsome and Dissolute, the Queen, Marie Leycinska is an old Dowdy, the Dauphin is like a Skeleton, ¶ the Royal Daughters are plain and Clumsy, and the Royal Infants are sickly. Versaille is magnificent to a degree, but I was astounded indeed at the swarms of ill-looking mob in amidst all this splendour. Some sell their wares in the very

* Marie Josephe : Princess of Saxony.—Ed.

† Daughters of Louis XV.: Princesses Marie Adelaide Victoire, Sophie, and Louise Marie.—Ed.

‡ Afterwards Louis XVI.—Ed.

§ Afterwards Louis XVIII.—Ed.

‖ Afterwards Charles X.—Ed.

¶ The Dauphin died in the following year.

antechamber of the King. The Picture Gallery, Orangerie and Gardens superb.

September 15th.

Ned declares that he is enjoying himself very well in this place. Indeed, he is abroad all day and night. He says 'tis the Liveliest Town he ever did see, and that the Boulevards are full of coffee houses, filles, music and noise and this needless to say, is exactly what pleases him most.

September 17th.

Cards and Supper at Lady H. French and English present. One of the latter, a stern old Dame by name Mrs. Forster, informed me that when She had performed the Grand Tour as a Child she had never lent back once! I swear I near replied: " Doubtless, Ma'am, that is why you are so stiff necked now." The french ladies talking of nothing but whether Rouge is permitted to the Devout by the Church, and of the scandal caused by some lady of high rank who has been conducting an Intrigue with a common Soldier. I am become a True Parisian now. I lie abed all Day and up all night

September 18*th.*

Madame de Brinoy escorted me in her coach to the Rue St. Honoré to see the Marvellous Temple of Fashion there. This street is the home of the Marchand des Modes, and we occupied ourselves for near an hour admiring the little Dolls and mannequins decked out in the newest Modes. These are sent all over the World, even to Constantinople and other Barbaric spots. Dinner at Madame de B.'s Hotel. 'Tis furnished most elegantly. The chairs covered with Rose Indian brocade. The carpet dove coloured with a Gold fringe. Also a superb rug composed entirely of Ermine fur—exquisite pictures by M. Greuze and Boucher. Sèvres china all sumptuous. Many guests present. Among others, Madame d'Egmont, Princesse Talmond, cousin to the Queen, and a Genteel young officer, Monsieur de Guys, cadet of a noble house and a Relative of Madame who paid me some little attention, fixing his fine dark eyes upon me all the meal which we eat in a Paved Hall with Frescoes and a pretty Fountain.

The conversation very Witty. Epigrams

and Bons Mots flying here and there. All Courtesy Itself to me except one lady, who asked me in a mincing voice if I did not live in a country where there was a Perpetual Fog and nothing to eat but Raw Meat and Baked Apples. Whereupon M. de Guys remarked quickly: " At all events Madame, I believe you will agree that the damp Climate and Apples have together given Mademoiselle a very beautiful Complexion " which I vow was immoderately Gallant of him.

September 21*st.*

A most Astounding incident occurred to-day. Returning with Madame Dupont from the Barbers we met in the Hall a young man of about 30 or so, attired neatly but " en bourgeois." I should not have observed him particularly but something in his entire appearance and figure seemed to me immoderately familiar. I gazed at him for several moments, attempting to call to mind where I had set eyes on him before. He returned my glance apparently no less Intrigued, at length bowed and passed out. Then I caught a glimpse of my own Person in a mirror, and it dawned upon me that the young man and me were as similar as Two Peas! I seized hold of Ned who entered at that moment and cried very agitated: " For Heaven's sake, Ned, who is that person who has this minute left us ? "

Whereupon he explained in a low voice that he was no other than our half-brother ! It seems in short, that my Father when in Paris on the Grand Tour years ago, fell violently enamoured of a pretty actress by name Clementina Denise and this was her son, hence the extraordinary likeness between us, both of us taking after Papa. Ned very vexed because my Father is determined to give the young man a large sum of money to enable him to obtain a commission in the French Army. It seems that Ned and my Father have had some sharp words about it, but I own that I feel a strong sympathy for this new relation of mine. To look at him I might suppose myself to be gazing into a mirror, while Ned with his carroty hair, which he inherits from Mamma, seems to me but a brother in name. Ned **warns** me to say nothing to Papa of this " Else, Miss," he said, " you will as likely as not get a Box on the Ear." This incident has caused me more thought than anything else on this tour.

September 23rd.

The French are a curious people indeed. To-day was invitated to a party with Mme. D'Agesseau and arriving found that the Lady of the House had just been brought to bed. This plan of Turning a Labour into an Entertainment is quite novel to me. Took refreshments and played cards in an adjourning room with a grand company of guests—till my Hostess was safely delivered of a daughter, whereupon I retired home.

October 2nd.

Have not wrote in this Journal for many days being in a mighty great Bustle these last few weeks. Yesterday Madame de Brinoy took me to visit Madame de Luxembourg. This lady was notorious for her gallantries in her youth; indeed Madame de B. tells me some wit made the following little verse upon her:

" Quand Boufflers * parut à la Cour
On croyait voir la Reine d'Amour ;
Chacun s'empressait à lui plaire
Et chacun l'avait à son tour."

which I think says all that need be said. But
now she is a leader of Society, arbiter of
Bon Ton, a Paragon of Propriety and 'tis
as essential to be presented at L'Hotel de
Luxembourg as at Versaille. In short her
Sins are forgiven her. She is a small, quiet
old lady, attired simply and modestly without
a jewel and you would never suspect she had
been such a great Rake. Madame de B.
accounts for her great Succés and the Merit
she has acquired in her old age, by her prodigious Sang Froid. A great number of the
Beau Monde present. It would seem that
there is no such thing as old Age in France,
for women of more than 60 are as Frivolous,
as gaily dressed and as sprightly as young
females. Madame de Brinoy, though she
has indeed a youthful Air, laughs mercilessly
at these Evergreens as she names them.

* The Maréchale de Luxembourg was the Duchesse de
Boufflers before she remarried.—Ed.

" At my age," she declared merrily, " a woman should be given up to Meditation. Indeed, I myself find great Consolation in thinking of the Sins I might have committed but have not."

Monsieur de Guys present, and to my surprise Monsieur de Belisle with as philosophical an air as ever. He hastened forward at the sight of me but I had a Malicious Joy in showing favour to Monsieur de Guys which I believe vexed him. Monsieur de G. is a captivating Fellow, elegant, witty, with vast superiority of parts. We conversed together for some time on the state of France. In his opinion the K.* should be deposed. " That cursed Butcher's Daughter † thank Heaven, is dead," he declared, " but you will see we shall soon be cursed with yet another money drinking wanton."

He abhors the Jesuits and is deeply solicitous for the Poverty of the Peasants.

" We are dancing on a Precipice," he declared, " but I can see no end to it all."

* King ? Monsieur de Guys was a bold young man.—ED.
† Madame de Pompadour.—ED.

He spoke also with scorn of the nobles of M. de Belisle's kind, who preach Revolution and Freedom and at the same moment send peasants to the Gallies for Trifling misdemeanours.

All this Serious Talk accompanied by Doux Yeux. Madame de Brinoy thinks highly of this young man.

October 3rd.

Papa attends Madame Geoffrin's * salons. Her Lundis are for the Artistic and her Wednesdays for the Literati. He declares that he meets very Cultured persons there and diverts himself prodigiously, but thank Heaven I have ended with all Philosophy, being engaged in pursuits more suitable for my age! Madame G. is a Bourgeoise, and not in society and will not permit women at her Reunions, and I think she is wise, for conversations upon Atheism and the famous Encyclopædia are more suitable for old men in their Dotage than young and pretty females. It seems that the other night some guest read from their works, and glancing up perceived that the Entire Company were

* The famous salonnière.—ED.

dozing, which does not say great things for the liveliness of it all.

To-day received a basket of late Roses from Monsieur de Guys and concealed among the Blooms a little note very prettily worded, assuring me that he received more pleasure from my Society than from that of any other Woman he knows, and saying some other vastly Pleasant things about my Person and Mind. I am not so vain as to Flatter myself that all this Praise is True, but I will own that this Graceful and yet Respectful Homage is very Gratifying at a moment when my heart is Aching at Mr. A.'s Perfidy. Apropos of that man, I have wrote him a short sharp letter in case my first note was mislaid on route, and I pray that this may bring him to his Senses.

October 5th.

A packet of English books from Monsieur de Guys, for I complained to him the other day that I had nothing to read. Among others Mr. Hume, Richardson and Mr. Walpole's " Castle of Otranto." Ned, who I believe has found himself a mistress by his

Lively Air, declares that Monsieur de G. is catched by me.

October 6th.

Cards at Madame de B. Met Monsieur de G. who would not depart from my side all the time. Madame de B. winks at me merrily about this.

October 7th.

Monsieur de G. has presented me with a charming little dog named Chloe. 'Tis the Genteelest, Sprightliest animal I ever set eyes on, and will console me for the loss of my dear Victor. Apropos of dogs, on the bridges here, the Shoeblacks cry at one: " Ici on tond les chiens et coupe les Oreilles aux Chiens et Chats," but I will not permit my little Chloe to be snipped even to be Modish.

October 9th.

Marie Bonheur brought me a short curious little note to-day. 'Twas in French and un-signed, to the effect that someone more worthy of my Favour than that Foppish little Officer (Monsieur de G. ?) was prepared to lay his Homage at my Feet and so on, calling me "ma belle Divine Fleur Irlandaise," " adorable Mademoiselle," and other foolish Terms of Endearment. To my mind it must be either wrote by a Lunatic or some Fool, wishing to play a jest on me. The french are very Partial to Hoaxes of this kind.

Marie Bonheur can explain nothing, except that it was delivered by a Lacquais de Louage. Very droll and mystifying.

October 11*th.*

To the opera with Madame de Brinoy. Wore my Rose Brocade and carried a Posy of Artificial Flowers which are the Mode here. She fetched me in her Coach which is Elegant like all she possesses, and has running footmen and Danish Hounds accompanying it. We were delayed for several minutes in a narrow street, whilst her Coachman quarrelled with another driver. She tells me that he is very particular as to Precedence, and would rather Risk overturning the Coach than give place to an Equipage of lesser rank. She herself is utterly indifferent to matters of this kind except when at Court. I informed her that Domestics were equally Odious in England, and recounted Paddy's Wicked Behaviour on the Bath Road. The music at the Opera poor, but the scenery sumptuous. Mademoiselle de Mesnils is the modish actress of the hour. Monsieur de Guys came to our box and stayed a great time conversing most tenderly with me. I wish to Heaven Mr. A. could know I have found another Beau.

October 12th.

Supped at Madame de Mirepoix. Saw Madame d'Harcourt as fair, as Languishing as ever she was. The lady has not the Strength now to lift a cup to her Lips or pull a bell rope—a lacquais must do it for her. Monsieur de G. very agreeable. Much diverted this morning at a street brawl below my Boudoir window. A woman emptied a Pail of Rubbish on the Head of a Priest, and then Lud! what a to do and yells and curses.

October 16th.

It is with the Deepest Melancholy that I take up my Pen to record the events of this Unhappy Day. I went to visit dear Madame de Brinoy this morning. I found her at her Toilette surrounded by Acquaintances and Tradespeople. After a while she dismissed them and I observed that she was in a state bordering on tears. With a silent look of Grief she handed me a letter from Madame de Guys, the mother of my poor friend, near Distraught, and announcing that her son has been sent to the Bastile by a Lettre de Cachet. At first on perusing this Melancholy News, I was Ignorant enough to imagine that my Unlucky Admirer had been thrown into prison for debt, and tearing off my Pearls, I offered them to Madame crying:—" We must make every effort to obtain his release," but Madame de Brinoy explained, with tears in her eyes, that this Dastardly business was the result of some Political crime or Indiscretion on my poor friend's part. What a vile country, where such injustices can be committed, and oh gracious heaven, what a Cruel ending to our Happy Friendship ! Madame de B. hurried off to visit the Unfortunate Young Gentleman's Mother, and left me here. Have spent the Day in Deep Dejection. My father and Ned very Solicitous, and Papa means to consult our Ambassador about this business, but I fear 'tis all in vain. I will

be Honest and confess that Monsieur de Guys
has not, and never could arouse in my bosom
the Passionate Love which I even now feel
for Mr. A., but nevertheless I have a Warm
Regard and Affection for him.   How can
I fail to be Frantic at the Frightful Fate that
has overtaken him ?

October 17th.
    Passed a Sleepless Night.   Am deeply de-
jected.   Have nothing but distaste at the
thought of participating in the many parties
and routs I have been invited to, but as Ned
rightly remarks, If I display my Distress too
ardently, everyone will Immediately conclude
that I am poor Monsieur de Guy's chère Amie.

November 1st.
    I see I have not wrote for a great long time.
These last two weeks has been little else but
a Weary Racket of Entertainments.   The
sad misfortune which overtook my poor
friend has stolen all joie de Vivre from me,
and I do not now enjoy these same gaieties.
I cannot say how I have missed his agreeable
countenance and elegant person at these
assemblies.   The thought of him deprived

of Freedom, and all that renders life dear, has embittered my stay in Paris, and I shall be happy to depart for Switzerland. Have learnt also that these Parisians are monstrously Selfish and Unfeeling beneath their masks of Courtesy and wit. Monsieur de G.'s imprisonment caused needless to say, a prodigious stir at first among his acquaintances, and all were highly indignant, but a few days passed and a Novel Topic became all the mode. All were laughing over the Scandal caused by some Cardinal or other who has been found to have a young female in his retinue disguised as a secretary in a Soutane, and so Monsieur de G. is forgot. I venture to mention the poor young gentleman to Monsieur de Tasse the other day whereupon he cried: "Oui Mademoiselle, c'est bien triste mais on n'en parle plus." Could anything be more Barbarous?

Last night a highly odious thing occurred to me. Ned and me and Madame Dupont went to the Opera. Papa being sick with the Gout. Half way through Ned spied a well-known courtezan, he is very catched by, and hastened to speak to the creature, leaving me alone save for Madame Dupont, who was asleep. Was mightily surprised when a second later Monsieur de Belisle entered my box, and sitting down by me without more ado began to make the most frantic love to me. Was so astounded that I remain mum like a Fool, whereupon he seized my hand and covered it with kisses. This vexed me furiously for I cannot abide a man with a badly turned leg,* so I rose very angry, roused Madame D. and hastened away. The reprobate had the impudence to follow me even to my coach with Passionate Protestations, which to my Intense Mortification made the Bystanders laugh, and as I stepped in, the Insolent Wretch said: " I believe you are amoureuse of that Idiot in the Bastille." This enraged me and I slammed the door in his face, pulled the cord and away we went splattering the Monster's fine coat with mud. These frenchmen are more licentious than could be imagined. Mr. A. is a Hermit beside them. My father mad with Ned for having abandoned me in this manner, and

* This remark seems somewhat obscure.—Ed.

threatens to run Monsieur de B. through if he ventures near us.

November 5th.

I'll own I have reason to be grateful to Providence for I am convinced that I am a very Great Fool, and but for Heaven's special protection might be ruined through my own Folly. In short, last night I indulged in a Monstrously Foolish adventure which near proved disastrous. All the talk among the ladies of late has been of Alchemists and magic crystals, and I have for some time had an inclination to visit one of these Magicians, and see their wonders for myself. Marie Bonheur learning of my desire declared that she knew of a certain Italian Seer by name Signor Orlando, who could read the future marvellously well, and who was frequented by all the Beau Monde. She promised to make a Rendezvous for me at this Man's house last night. I will own I was drawn into this silly affair by the hope of learning some news of Mr. A. and Monsieur de Guy. I then thought for Greater Security and also to make the adventure more Diverting, that I would attire myself as a young man. In short, I took a green satin suit of Neds, and with Marie Bonheur's assistance cut it down to suit my figure. I tied my hair in a periwig and armed with a rapier and cocked hat, and looking a very proper young Beau, set off in a chair with Marie B. Arrived at the place, I was bowed up by a Negro Page to a dark room furnished with serpents and skulls. Waited for some time, Marie Bonheur having vanished, and began to be Uneasy. All on a sudden the page came in again. " In here, Monsieur please," says he and pulls back a curtain. I hastened into an inner chamber and came face to face with the detestable De Belisle, who grabbed me in his arms and began embracing me like a Lunatick. I will not trouble to write down all the indelicate and Abominable things he said. In a great fright I yelled and kicked and screamed. Thank the Lord, I had the good sense to draw my sword and deliver him a blow in the chest with the hilt, which made him leave go. Whereupon I ran out of the room, downstairs and into the road, and jumped into a chair and so home. Never has such an agitating thing occurred to me before. Papa knows nothing of this escapade, and never shall, if I can help it. The odious maid has never returned to-day. 'Tis plain she was in his pay, and besides playing me this Wicked Trick, she has stolen my Plum brocade, but 'tis not vastly becoming to me, and am happy to be out of this business too so easily.

November 7th.

I feel I must note down a diverting little sequel to the Alarming affair t'other night. To-day Ned, poor youth, decided to wear his green suit, which I had replaced by stealth, and was prodigiously Put Out at finding it too tight! The buttons strained to breaking point over his chest, and the sleeves too short. Needless to say I have not vouchsafed an explanation, and 'tis accounted for by the idea that he has grown Stout on french cooking. I laughed till I near split.

November 19th.

Very busied this last week with preparation for our prodigious lengthy journey. The Hateful Marie has been replaced by a Swiss

girl named Nanette, who seems Honest
enough.   At all events she is excessively
Plain.   One of the valets very drunk, so we
have found another.   The journey to Switzerland will be very severe in this season, my
acquaintances declare we shall never reach
there alive.   Have purchased a beautiful
hood and cloak, lined with Fur, to keep off
the cold.   Also very elegant.

November 22nd.

We are to break our journey by lying at
the Abbé d'Autune.   Tom who was ac-
quainted with him in Paris some years ago,
has sent us Letters of Recommendation to
him.   We inquired at his Town residence,
but they informed us that he has not visited
Paris for many years now, and lives altogether
in the Country, near Chalons.   It will be
agreeable to have this opportunity of observing true country life, for Chanteloup was
magnificent, and in no way Bucolic.

November 27th.

Ned has purchased a Genteel little Mouse-
coloured Donkey, who is to run behind our
coach.

November 28th.

My last day in this Gay Cruel City. Our antechamber all in a Bustle with lacquais bringing Lettres de Congé. An affecting parting with Madame de Brinoy, who presents me with a sweet miniature of herself, set in pearls. She begs me to visit her on my return. Ned very vexed at leaving Paris. He seems to have an Intrigue with a lady of great fascination. At all events he is in a very Ill Humour.

December 7th.

Here we find ourselves at the frontier at Gex, and here we shall remain till we have recovered somewhat from the fatigues of our journey. My father suffers from sciatica, Ned has a cold in the Head, and I am for some reason or other excessively Low Spirited; melancholy at leaving France, yet unwilling to remain there, and Profoundly Uneasy apropos of Mr. A. Our journey was Damnably Unpleasant. The country we passed through was often Beautiful, but the incessant rain prevented me from admiring it. Inns vile, and one night I was obliged to have my bed in a kind of outhouse. Our

visit to the Abbé though excessively vexatious
to Papa was, now I come to think on it, the
drollest thing that has ever occurred to me,
and I shake with Laughter every time 'tis
mentioned.   After a lengthy day over bad
roads we reached to our amazement a very
Decayed looking house, more like a Ruin
than a Gentleman's Residence; finding ourselves in a courtyard filled with Rubbish, we
concluded that we had mistaken our way,
but the door opened and a Strange Figure
attired in a Dirty Soutane, and carrying a
gun, emerged and glared at us like a wild
beast.   This it seemed was our host the Abbé
himself.   He greeted us in a Surly manner,
declaring that he was occupied shooting
wolves and seemed at first inclined to leave
us out in the Rain, at length led us indoors—
all very amazed at this Curious Reception.
Never shall I forget the amazing ménage we
found ourselves in.   The house was filthy
dirty, devoid of any ordinary Comforts.
Seated in the hall were two men playing
cards, as Dirty and Unkempt as our host,
ill-mannered country Boors who did not
even salute us, but continued to converse

in Loud Tones. This embarrassed us, but
more was to come. A door opened and two
females came out, both painted abominably,
and attired in Tawdry and Immodestly cut
garments. They seemed angry at the sight
of us, and drew back. In short 'twas easy
to perceive that they were nothing better
than common trollops. This then was the
home of the Benevolent and cultured Abbé,
where we had fondly hoped to lie the night!
'Twas all so Droll and Unexpected that I near
broke out laughing, but my father became
Purple with rage at finding himself in such a
low place, and when our host was out of
hearing, he declared that we must depart
instantly. Ned and me however were near
dead with travelling, and begged him to
remain, which he did, on condition that I
should go at once to my chamber with Mme.
Dupont, and bolt my door. We had a
miserable repast of sour wine and soup, my
Father and Ned standing over me in such
a manner that none of our disreputable
fellow guests were able to approach me, if
indeed they had desired to do so, for they
remained drinking in a corner, and plainly

making lewd jokes about us, and me in particular. Madame D. and me were escorted by the Abbé, who all this time had not addressed a word to us, to our chamber. Not a sign I should say of a Domestic. To reach it we were obliged to cross an open yard in the Rain, and so arrived wet and Shivering in a Bare Room with not a stick of Furniture, but a bed, a chair, and a table. We barred ourselves into this Delectable Apartment, and seeing no sign of water to wash with, lay fully clothed upon our bed, which to add to our Discomfort, gave way under our Combined Weights, and had to be propped up with the Chair. Needless to remark we did not sleep very soundly in this fashion, more especially as Loud Sounds of Merriment came from Below stairs, and also we were pestered by Lice. We were however unmolested though at about midnight a Heavy Body fell against our door, which we trembling concluded was a Drunken Guest retiring to bed. Papa and Ned woke us at Dawn, and we departed without setting eyes again on our Host and his friends. Papa more Vexed and Furious at this affair than

I have ever seen him before.   Ned and me
inclined to laugh at it all, but my father in a
terrible Passion.   He declares that he would
like to hang Tom for sending us to such a
place—" My daughter lying in the same
house as two wantons " he cried at least 20
times in a fury.   He declares that he was a
Fool to bring a girl on a Tour like this, and
swore at me when I told him my Reputation
could survive it.   We inquired at our first
opportunity for Particulars of our strange
host, and an Innkeeper soon made all plain
to us.   The Abbé, though doubtless quite
Comme il Faut when Tom was in France, is
now a Notorious Personage.   Some 10 years
since he was banished from Paris for having
wrote a Blasphemous and Obscene novel.
He was in short Unfrocked and completely
disgraced.   He retired to the country, where
he has lived a Life of Shocking Vice.   No one
will venture near him, except Disreputable
men and *filles de joie* from the neighbouring
town.

What could be more Ludicrous than that
we should find ourselves in such a place ?
This morning Ned and self laughed over it,

till we wept. I must own this Droll business has been a Welcome Diversion to my low spirits. I dreamt last night that Mr. A. was in the Bastille chained hand and foot.

VI

SWITZERLAND

VI

SWITZERLAND

December 10th.—Lausanne.

I am firmly persuaded that this is the most
Idyllic country in the World. We had no
sooner crossed the frontier into Switzerland
than my spirits rose prodigiously. The air
seemed more Salubrious, the scenery more
Smiling, the inhabitants and houses cleaner,
happier, and more prosperous than those we
had left behind in France.

As I write from our hotel I can View from
my open window what must surely be one
of the Finest Spectacles in Europe. The
famous Lac de Leman lies before me Blue
and Sparkling in the winter sunshine, sailing
vessels and other small craft gliding to and fro
upon its Dimpling Surface, while upon the
opposite shore are a Superb Range of Snow
Capped and Craggy mountains, which seem
the very guardians, stern but kindly, of this
lovely country. No scene could be more
calculated to cheer and yet elevate the mind.
As I gaze upon these Awe Inspiring Rocks
I am more than ever convinced of the Power

of Heaven as demonstrated in Nature, and the Comparative Frivolity of our Human Desires and Efforts. The Food here is Excellent. 'Tis indeed a land flowing with milk and Honey. Nanette, who is overjoyed at finding herself in her Belle Suisse once more, brings me a Delicious cup of chocolate every morning and I dare swear I shall soon become quite stout. Indeed, I believe if I had stayed in France much longer I should have lost all my looks. We stayed at Geneva but a few days, for 'twas a large, Melancholy town, full of Pastors and excessively cold, and we were told that the air here is Finer and the Society more English. To-day walking abroad to examine the Town, I heard so many English voices around me that I might have imagined myself in Derby once more. 'Tis Delightful to hear one's own Tongue again. The streets here are monstrously hilly and Ill paved. I shall spend a fortune on shoes. A fine Cathedral and Castle here.

December 14*th.*

A pacquet of letters arrived from England. Ned received one from dear Cousin Noll, portions of which he read out aloud to us.

At the end Ned cried: " Why, Sister, your villainous Admirer is at large!" but I gave him a sharp kick under the table, and Papa looked up sternly, which quickly silenced him. He informed me, as soon as Papa was away, that Mr. A. had left Ireland these last two months, and is in London with Sir James Ford. This news has agitated me more than I can say. It explains in some measure Mr. Ancaster's silence which has so Pained me, and yet I cannot imagine why, or with what Motives he has taken this step. How am I to communicate with him ? What is he about ? These and a hundred other doubts exercise my Troubled Mind. From what I have observed of London, 'tis full of Snares for a young man of Mr. A.'s hot disposition, and great good looks. I can only pray he will remain Faithful. I myself received to my Joy a letter from dear Lydia D'Arcy or Lydia Franklin as I should now call her. She is still at her Aunt's residence, but Fortune seems inclined to smile upon her. Her husband has lately become, through the death of a relative, second Heir to a Baronetcy, and so there is every Hope that her parents will be reconciled to the Marriage. Of this I am heartily glad. She begs me to send her some little Cadeau from Italy, which I shall most certainly do, and also inform her of the latest Parisian Modes. She declares she will name her infant Cleone if it proves a Female. We have moved to good Appartements in the Rue du Grand Chêne.

December 16th.

Several of the best English families resident here have paid us visits, and invited us to their parties.

This morning on the stairs a tall young gentleman with green eyes came up to me and bowing very respectfully, said that he had heard my name by chance, and was I any relation to Ned Knox whom he had known at Eton? When I owned that I was Ned's sister, he presented himself as Mr. Richard Dickinson from Co. Cork. Ned very delighted at meeting this ancient school-fellow. He is a very lively, genteel young man, and is out here to learn the language, though as he confesses himself, he has not spoken a word of french yet. I think he will prove an agreeable addition to our acquaintance. We took chocolate with him in the town, and he introduced Ned to a young Swiss lady shopping with her Mother. This young Miss, whom Ned appeared greatly to admire, is by name Mlle. Henriette-Cecile Pochon. She belongs to one of the genteelist families here. She is fair and handsome, her features agreeable and her person well formed. She responded to Ned's advances, but it is easy to see that she is modest and virtuous, and I do not know how Ned will care for that.

December 21*st*.

I am no less pleased with this place than when I first arrived. The admirable Simplicity of the Society here is most agreeable after Paris. There are many aristocratic families here, but I observe none of that Hauteur which is so Odiously noticeable in the French Nobility. In this blessed republic all are equally free, happy and self-respecting. Noble, peasant and bourgeois only vie with each other in serving the community. Still more marvellous, speech is utterly free and unrestrained. No Bastille threatens the Fortunate Swiss. The abuses of the French Monarchy are discussed and condemned at the literary and philosophical debates, all with the greatest boldness. Ideas, new and often startling are exchanged. The Rights of Individuality are proclaimed. Escorted by Ned and Mr. D. I have attended several reunions amongst our Swiss acquaintances, and I drew considerable applause upon myself the other evening by describing the poverty of the french peasant or of much of it as I had observed.

If I had made half these remarks in France, doubtless I would have been thrown into prison like poor Monsieur de Guys. The air of liberty which we breathe here is intoxicating, and there is a danger of throwing prudence to the winds and propounding wild and extravagant ideas, for everything one says is listened to with flattering attention. Lausanne is at present crowded with young Englishmen on their travels. Papa says that they are a Crew of Idle Young Puppies wasting their parents' substance; when they should be applying themselves to studying. But in my opinion they make the Society very lively.

Ned and me both out all day to parties

where we dance and play cards. All the diversions here very innocent. The weather continues to be fine, though somewhat cold. This town is very clean after Paris.

December 25th.

Though absent from Ireland and David A., to-day has been one of the most agreeable Christmases I have spent. The weather very fine and sunny and indeed they say that this is the mildest winter they have known for some years. The streets thronged with the bourgeoisie in their best clothes, all very merry and exchanging compliments of the season. Church, followed by a large dinner, which we gave here to our English acquaintances. Gifts were exchanged. Papa gave me " Excellent Discourses on Life and Death " by Dr. Giles Witherspoon, and a pair of red shoes with gold buckles. Ned, a china comfit box with apologies, for he is short of funds. Mr. D. presented me with a pretty pink embroidered neck-ribbon for dear Chloe. I gave Papa a Prayer Book elegantly bound, and a pair of fine lace ruffles to Ned. Many toasts were drunk, amongst others, The charming Miss Cleone—

this to my vast embarrassment—and the Swiss Republic, in honour of our native guests.

Mlle. Pochon has had the goodness to give me a history of Venice which I shall study, doubtless with profit. I have offered her a length of fine Belfast lawn which most happily I had amongst my wardrobe, for I had not a sou left.

January 3rd, 1765.

Delighted to receive a charming letter from dear Mme. de Brinoy. She expresses most kindly her regret at my departure and envies me my visit to this Country. She gave me a diverting account of a visit she has recently made to a country-house near Paris. The guests there were all young and immoderately lively, and spent their days and nights playing off tricks on each other, dropping salt in the coffee, pepper in the snuff, digging holes in the garden walks and so on. " At my age," she wrote, " one is not overjoyed to find a frog in one's bed." Apropos of poor Monsieur de Guys—she says that his friends are still active on his behalf, and she has strong hopes that they will obtain his release, which I heartily pray they may.

January 5th.

I perceive that I never truly appreciated the Beauties of Nature before coming to this country, where we talk of little else. The Swiss delight in the majestic and sublime scenery which surrounds them. Mme. Pochon has, indeed, offered a gilded wreath of laurel leaves as reward for the most elegant poem on the Lake of Geneva, and though I shall not compete for this, I am every day learning the Infinite Superiority of Natural Beauty over the Gilded Hollow Luxury which is the work of Man's Hands.*

Yesterday my Father, Mr. Johnston, Ned, Mlle. Pochon, Mr. Dickinson and me, made an excursion to the village of Clarens immortalised by Monsieur Rousseau in his sublime work " La Nouvelle Heloïse." This trip partook more of the nature of a Pilgrimage than a mere Excursion. Mr. J. and Mlle. P. in particular being ardent admirers

* The Editor has here deleted two closely written pages in the same strain. The rapturous priggishness of this period of the eighteenth century with regard to nature is too well known to need further comment

of the celebrated writer. We performed most
of the journey by chaise and the day being
excessively fine and calm, we embarked near
Clarens in a small boat, rowing by turns.
Mr. Dickinson and I rowed side by side,
my Father and Mr. J. in front with their
backs to us. My oar slipped in my unskilled
hand, throwing me violently against Mr. D.,
who took the occasion to kiss me. 'Twas
somewhat sudden, but so respectful that I did
not demur. Papa perceived something in
the clear water, for he turned abruptly, but
it was all finished then.

Ned and Mlle. Pochon, who were reading
" La Nouvelle Heloïse " in the stern of the
boat, observed this little transaction. Ned
laughed, but I fancied I perceived an expression of Reproof on the face of the Miss.
There is no question that though in every
respect the Swiss are a vastly Respectable
race, they are lacking in Sprightliness. We
examined the village of Clarens with interest,
and walked for some time in the Renowned
Bosquet de Julie.* Mlle. P. moved to tears
at the thought of the unhappy lovers. Mr.

*Byron and Shelley visited this same spot many years later.—ED.

Johnston also wept. Mr. D. showed great
solicitude and led me away, and we plucked
grasses and sweet smelling herbs. I have
pressed the latter in my prayer-book. The
scenery round us could be described by these
words of Petrarch, which can be found in the
" Nouvelle Heloïse:"

  ' " Aux lieux des palais, des pavillons, des
     théâtres: les chênes, les noirs sapins,
     les hêtres s'élancent de l'herbe verte au
     sommet des monts et semblent élever
     au ciel avec leurs têtes les yeux et
     l'esprits des mortels."

We dined at an Inn and ate an admirable
omlette. All very light-hearted. For our
greater diversion we named each other after
the characters of the novel. Thus Mlle.
Pochon was " Julie," I was " Claire," Mr. D.
was " Saint Preux " and so on. Was filled
with admiration at the peasants who are tall,
handsome and possessed of a natural breeding
and easiness of manners. Their dwellings
are clean and neat, nothing more unlike
France could be imagined.

January 8th.

I have been begged to join the Société du Printemps which is a coterie of Young Ladies who meet together for Amusement and Instruction. The Male Sex are not excluded from this gathering, but there are no Duennas and 'tis astonishing with what decorum and propriety these same parties are conducted. Mr. A., in this company would be a wolf among lambs.

January 9th.

Mme. Pochon had the complaisance to escort us to Ferney to pay our homages to the illustrious philosopher, Monsieur de Voltaire. The great man received us in a chintz dressing-gown, with a flow of brilliant wit. Sometimes affable, more often peevish. To tell truth, he reminded me of nothing so much as a chattering old magpie. But we listened silent, with that Respect which is due to Genius, however Wearisome it may be. He related a variety of droll tales and spoke with immoderate abuse of Religion. This same subject it would seem is something of a mania with him. We had an excellent repast of fish and roast meat, and were later escorted by his niece, Mme. Denys, an ugly, silly female, round the house and village. Monsieur de Voltaire has showed the benevolence which he undoubtedly possesses beneath his Irascible and Odious manner in constructing dwellings for the peasants. Monsieur de Voltaire's house is simple but comfortable and genteel. It was filled with guests like an Inn. Amongst others an agreeable young painter by name Monsieur Charles. Mme. Pochon says his true name is the Chevalier de Boufflers.* The country around Ferney resembles England but for a superb view of lake and mountains. Monsieur de Voltaire cultivates bees and cows. Papa thought highly of his farming qualities. The only disagreeable incident I have to record of this day's business, is that Ned, like the Damned Fool he is, attempted to engage in a controversy with our Illustrious host on the Influence of Religion on the Female Mind. The few words Monsieur de Voltaire vouchsafed to Ned in reply were of such a Savage and Mortifying nature that

* Madame Pochon was probably correct. The celebrated Chevalier de Boufflers was in Switzerland and staying incognito with Voltaire about this date.—Ed.

I near choked with Shame. We stayed the night here at a very good Inn in the Bourg de Four. We came to Geneva by barque from the village of Ouchy, to return to-morrow by the same route.

January 12*th.*

A most agreeable party at the Société du Printemps. Several young ladies recited Odes of their own composition in praise of the Lakes, Mountains and other Beauties of Nature. Some more elegantly turned than others, but all displaying Sensibility and Refinement. Am astounded to observe how accomplished these Swiss Ladies are. Mlle. Pochon talked of nothing but a young couple of her acquaintance but lately wedded, who have retired to a chalet above the Lake and renounced town life and Civilisation in general. This Monsieur and Madame Écuyer, although wealthy, live in Admirable Simplicity, milking their own cows, washing their own linen, in short, performing all Household duties without assistance. They eat no meat, nourishing themselves almost entirely upon greens, and, according to Mlle. P. are as Happy as possible. So joyous do they find their rural solitude that they have no inclination to return to Lausanne, but nevertheless are happy to receive visitors. A great many of their acquaintances have been to visit them this summer, and all exclaim at their bliss. To my mind nothing could be more Delightful than this kind of life. Would to Heaven that I could retire to some such Peaceful retreat with A Congenial Companion and pass my Days in Innocent Bucolic Occupations. After 2 Seasons spent in the gaieties of the Beau Monde, I am convinced of the Emptiness and Hollowness of what is termed Polite Society.

January 30*th.*

The days pass in the agreeabliest manner possible here. Ned has a fencing master and music-master two days a week, Whilst I am engaged in studying Italian and Latin with Mr. Dickinson.

We have not, however, renounced more sprightly occupations! Last night we attended a fine Ball. Mr. D. and I danced a prodigious number of Minuets and French Country Dances. A vast number of English present.　Amongst others Sir John and Lady Bower, Mrs. Templeton and her two captivating daughters.　The elder Georgina is distinguished by the symmetry of her arms and shoulders.　The younger Elizabeth, has, I admit, a killing enough pair of brown eyes, but her expression to my mind is insipid. Danced with Monsieur de Blonay, who owns, I am told, a fine château on the french shore of the Lake at Evian.　He tells me that Amphion is a very fashionable bathing place now, and counselled Papa to visit it in the Spring for his gout.

Mr. Dickinson declares that some of the young English Gentlemen in Geneva have angered the Genevois who are excessively prudish, by their follies and excesses.　Apropos of Mrs. Templeton, her absurd french is the laugh of the Town.　The other evening at a party she was exclaiming on the cold of this country, and how she was constrained to sleep between two mattresses for warmth, but as she committed the amazing error of saying: "Il faut que je me couche entre deux *matelots*," the entire company was thrown into fits of merriment.　I vow that if the poor lady had made the same blunder in Paris, her reputation would have been gone for ever.

February 14*th.*

Ned, Mr. D. and me escorted yesterday by Mlle. Pochon to wait on the Ecuyers in their rural retreat. The weather being at length favourable to this much hoped for excursion. The first part of the journey was by chaise. We were then conveyed up the Mountain Slopes, in sleighs. Monstrously cold, and I was near frozen notwithstanding my fur Cape. The E.'s Chalet is situated in a Commanding position overlooking the Lake, but not, thank the Lord, at an excessively high altitude, else should have been perished *en route*. Mlle. Pochon assured us that in the warm season the surroundings are Delicious, but now all under snow and a chill wind.

We found Monsieur Ecuyer brushing the Snow from the doorstep. Their welcome scarcely more warm than the weather, and it seemed that our visit was ill-timed, for our Hosts had been unable to lay in their usual provisions. They appeared vexed that we

o

had not carried some viands with us.　Mme.
Ecuyer an agreeable, thin young female
received us with amiability, but the repast
we were offered was poor to a degree, being
nothing but country bread and stewed roots.
Ned, with his fine, healthy appetite and love
of Roast Beef pulled a long face at such poor
stuff.　I near split with laughter to see his
air of chagrin.　Mme. E. waited on us all the
meal like a common domestic, her spouse
meanwhile declaiming on Monsieur Rousseau and the beauties of the Natural Life.

Observed that the poor lady's hands were
all red and swollen, doubtless the result of
washing dishes and floors in this inclement
weather.　The chalet commodious enough,
but not over clean and in a great state of
confusion.　We did not stay long, for Mlle.
Pochon and self were chattering with cold,
and the two young gentlemen had a sharp
dispute with Monsieur E. on the Morality
of Fox-Hunting.　Monsieur E. declaring it
was a sin to kill a poor dumb beast, Ned and
Mr. D. defending the Chase with ardour.
Monsieur Ecuyer to my mind an ill-tempered
man who cannot abide contradiction.　I vow

I would not be shut up with him in the mountains for all the world. We made our adieux with readiness. I observed carved over the threshold the following words in french:

" Here Abides Beauty without Luxury,
    Peace without Idleness and Love without
    Sensuality."

Mr. Dickinson whispered to me in his waggish manner: " Indeed, Ma'am, I have never yet known a man who could be Licentious on Herbs and Water ! "

Mlle. Pochon promised to wait on them in the Spring. " If," cried Ned rudely, " you are not frozen to death by then."

We refreshed ourselves with chocolate at an auberge, and never was drink more grateful.

March 16*th.*

'Tis with regret that I contemplate our departure from this Delightful Country where I have spent so many happy hours. Mlle. Pochon made a visit last year to her maternal aunt at Turin and declares to my surprise that she did not care for Italy. The towns she says are Dirty and Stinking, the inhabitants are Talkative and Untrustworthy. To-day Mr. Dickinson, who leaves to-morrow for Ireland came to pay his adieux to me. The young gentleman seemed somewhat agitated and sat for several hours conversing in a distracted manner. He declared that he had never been happier than during these last months in my society, and that life would seem very insipid when he could no longer see my charming countenance, and so on. At length he confessed that he had for some time been desirous of entering the Holy State of Matrimony, and I will own that I was fully expectant of a Declaration, when he ended all of a sudden: " Unhappily I have no Means but my Paltry Allowance, and even less Prospects, so I am unable to follow my Inclinations." Then pulling a piece of Eidelweiss from his waistcoat pocket he offered it to me, declaring that he had plucked it for me in the mountains, took a tender farewell and departed. I truly believe that the poor Youth is a trifle catched by me.

March 18*th.*

Am pained to have record that I had a

monstrously sharp quarrel with Ned to-day,
and thus broke my solemn vow made to
Papa.   I happened to fasten Mr. D.'s
Eidelweiss on my bodice.   Ned observed it
and informed me laughing that Mr. D. was
a damned liar and never climbed for it at all.
I maintained that he had, whereupon Ned
said in a provokingly rude manner: " My
poor Sister, I was with him when he purchased it from a peasant in this very city."
This threw me into a passion.   Doubtless,
'tis unreasonable but I am provoked at dis-
covering Mr. D.'s odious artifice.

VII

VENICE

VII

VENICE

April 2nd.

Have decided on the following new wardrobe for the Spring. Item. A buttercup silk, with red and green. White Moire gown, ruffled with pink Lilac Satin, and a Striped Peau de Soie. Pink and Apple Green Striped Satin with Feathers. Crimson Gros de Tour trimmed with Valencienne. Sky Blue Satin gown with Bouquets of Flowers with thick Ruching.

This with what I have should set me up genteely till Vienna. The Gentildonne here wear the neatest, prettiest costume imaginable, which I should like to imitate, viz: A three cornered hat worn over one side, a thick silk gown and over it all a zendaletto of black or white lace which is monstrously becoming to the face and form. Patches and perfumes used excessively here and Nanette informs me that the hairdressers are excellent.

Papa has purchased himself a new spring suit and as for Ned, he is ordering himself

new satin breeches and coats every moment.
Heaven knows who will pay for it all. The
Venetian ladies are monstrously pretty, and
run about the town as free as air, even the
Noblest born. One of them ogled Ned this
morning and he near fell from the Gondola
with joy. He thinks himself in Paradise.
Apropos of the gondola, 'tis a most convenient mode of conveyance and takes the
place of a chair. One would be very uneasy
without them with all this Plaguey Water.
We have a gondola with a fine Canopy. Our
gondolier wears a red Hat and puts me in
mind of Mr. A.

April 3rd.

To-day we paid our respects to several of
the Noble Families here. The great families
are the Moncenigo, the Gradenigos, Moro-
sini and many others. Was astounded at the
Magnificence of their Palaces. Hundreds
of apartments, and Papa says he doubts
if they have fewer than 9 gondolas and 50
servants in livery. The rooms hung with
damask and cut velvet. Even at Paris I
never saw such sumptuousness. They must
be prodigiously Wealthy. The Venetian

Ladies very affable and chattering about their lovers, the pains of confinement and clothes. They inquired eagerly of the latest modes in Paris. They offered me chocolate. All spoke french, happily, for my Italian is poor and halting. The mob have the strangest lisping dialect which I swear I shall never comprehend. Ned and me to the theatre last night, for the season ends on Maundy Thursday. They acted the " Diddone Abbadonata." The audiences conversed and laughed so loud before the curtain was opened that 'twas like Bedlam. A vast number of young nobles present in the Boxes with their mistresses. They spat on the mob below and conducted themselves in a very dégagé manner. The noble ladies some of them in very low dresses. In the tragic scene the heroine all on a sudden lifted her robes and danced a " furlana " * and sang a popular song.

A masked youth threw a posy of flowers at me. Laughed to find among the blooms a note and written in Italian : " This girl would

* Venetian dance.—ED.

make Love itself in Love." We eat ices and chocolate between whiles. Have purchased a black gauze veil for a marvellously low price in the Merceria.

April 4th.

The churches very frequented by Society during Lent, and I have peeped into Santa Maria Maggiore and San Marco to-day. To my mind St. Marks can in no way be compared to Westminster Abbey. 'Tis small and dark and has a exotick Papist air about it which does not please me, though I will own the gilding is fine. Sermons being declaimed in both these churches, the congregation meanwhile sticking on patches, yawning and making Love very comfortably. A young gentleman pinched my arm with the Sweetest Smile in the world.

Papa furious at my entering a Roman Church but I assure him that it cannot harm my soul as I do not comprehend a word of their Latin Gibberish. 'Tis diverting and the Music often Ravishing. Ned plays at rackets and goes fishing with the young nobles here.

April 5th.

Good Friday so I stayed indoors and read my Prayer Book.

April 6th.

All the Ladies here have Cavaliere Servants or Cicesbeo as they call them here, and I shall be démodé if I do not procure one by some means or other. Madame Caterina Dolfin who has the finest gold hair and blue eyes imaginable, informs me that they are not Lovers so much as Admirers and are very convenient for holding one's gloves and are even willing to assist at one's Toilette. Fear Papa would throw such an Admirer out of the house.

Am kept awake all night by the Traccasserie below my window. A Traghetto there and I hear a Hunchback telling stories to the neighbourhood, Gondoliers singing Tasso or serenading their Belles, in short a continual Chatter till Early Dawn. Papa says he will move to a quieter place.

April 7th.—Easter Sunday.

Ned and me watched a very Magnificent procession to St. Mark for High Mass. The

Doge in a Cambric hat and golden robes escorted by trumpeters and other Pomp. Observed that he kept his hat on even in the sacred building and this made Ned and me titter. A great crush, and the heat and odour of perfumes unbearable, so we went on to the Piazza and admired the Royal galley in the harbour. Apropos of the Doge, he is a Mocenigo. The Dogaressa Pisani Corner Mocenigo is they say, a very worthy lady.

April 9th.

Caught my dear Ned at his Pranks once more. Entered his room for a moment, and on departing inadvertently knocked over a screen which fell displaying a Pretty Little Slut in a striped petticoat. The wanton curtseyed to me and tripped out of the room, not in the least Abashed. Ned very vexed and informed me that she was not a Fille de Joie but a ballet dancer whom our gondolier has procured for him. He then declared that he adored Venetian women, who, in his opinion, were made for kisses, and would I please keep out of his room in future.

April 11th.

Never have I seen so many courtezans as

in this place. They run around as Bold as
Brass and are treated with as much Egards
as if they were women of fashion. They
walk on the Piazza hanging on the arms of
the Nobles, and every patrician's gondola
has one seated under the felze. Have even
seen a priest bring his Lady love to church
with him. Believe the Venetians do not
know what the word " shame " signifies.

Ned says the Nobles here are the poorest
spirited lot of Jackanapes he ever met.
When they are insulted they merely laugh,
and later hire an Assassin to revenge them.
Papa also declares that he is pestered all day
by Poverty Stricken aristocrats begging him
to give them money for the Ridotto.

In short they seem fit for nothing but
Licentious Amusements. Lud ! how Mr. A.
would despise such poor creatures.

April 12*th.*
Paddy and Stefano the Gondolier had a
fight to-day, and S. gave P. a black eye.
Paddy very melancholy at first at all this
water and no horses, but of late has taken to
rowing a Gondola. Madame Cecilia Zeno
T——n who is from all accounts a very

lighthearted gallant lady, escorted me out to-day in her gondola. She pointed out to me an excessively handsome old noble who passed us and cried " That old gentleman mon aimable enfant, is father to all the handsomest young people in Venice." Madame also made me laugh by recounting to me a diverting tale which is going the rounds this week. It seems that old Madame Guistina Qu——i, who is among the noblest patrician ladies in Venice, has always been mightily severe on the younger and frailer members of her sex. The other day the poor dame found that her tiring maid who has been in her service, undressed her and performed her toilette for these last ten years, was nothing but a Man in disguise ! All Venice is laughing at her Dismay, and needless to say not a soul will believe that he was not her lover.

Chloe is growing stout for the little wretch gorges itself on chocolate. My acquaintances each bring a sweetmeat for my cagnetta, as they call it, when they visit me at my Toilette.

April 15th.

Wrote a pretty little poem yesterday to

Madame Contarina Barbarigo's tabby cat, but I have used it as a curl paper by accident and I have forgot how it ran.

Apropos of cats, this morning I read in the Nuova Gazetta or some such journal that a cat belonging to the parish of San Gervasio and Potasio had given birth to three black and blue striped kittens. Hastened to the barber where I found half my acquaintances, but the prodigious Cats had died overnight to our vast Chagrin. We took chocolate at Florians on the Piazza, and I heard all the Scandal. It seems among other things that Sir William Brock is ruining himself at the Ridotto. A vast amount of Theatre gossip, but it has slipped my mind. Listened to the organ in St. Marks. A gallant in a crimson cloak slipped a three cornered note into the bosom of my gown. The usual request for a rendezvous. Ned and me visited the Ridotto to-day. 'Tis the Gambling Saloon here and a strange sight indeed. All the gamblers masked, a noble at the head of every table of which there are 80 or 90. The place lighted by silver candles. All plainly in a vast state of agitation, yet all play in silence, their countenances alone demonstrating the uneasiness of their minds. Every kind of person here. Nobles and ladies of high rank, courtezans, beggars, Negros, Turks, Jews and cutpurses.

Ned informs me that the other night a noble staked his Mother and lost. I told him teasingly that I wished I could do the same with him !

April 16*th.*
A wedding shortly to take place between members of the Zeno and Conti families. Papa and me were invited to the bride's residence to admire the gifts she has received. A great banquet, and we spent over two hours examining her garments and jewels. Never have I seen such a wardrobe before. At least a score or more of gowns, all of rich materials. A profusion of gold and silver brocade, velvet, linen, fans, buckles, shoes, lace and embroidery. Among her gowns I call to mind in particular a superb costume of silver satin embroidered in silver and flowers, a cloak of rose coloured velvet trimmed with ermine and with a jewelled clasp, a mauve camelot riding habit em-

broidered in gold and silver, a gown of pale
blue damask with bodice of beaver, a wrapper
of blue velvet trimmed with Canadian
marten, and all this for a Pale, thin girl of 16.
It seems that many Venetians separate or
obtain annulment after their marriages, and
so as like as not, all this fine wardrobe will
be wasted.   Purchased to-day in the Merceria a white fan with gold sequins, a neck-
lace for Cary and a lace cloak for Lydia
Franklin.   This cost me 15 sequins.*

Saw in the Piazza a Russian officer with a
blue and gold uniform, and a Turk in a
Turban.   Also observed a lady with a
modish muff of leopard skin.   I should like
to have the same.   The Piazza is so crowded
one can scarce move in it.   I believe the mob
live in it.   Have persuaded Papa to dress
our gondolier in a red silk jacket and sash
and white shoes.   The gondoliers at the
traghetto wear plumes in their Hats.

April 17*th.*

A musical party at the Bonfandins.   An
abbé played superbly on the Harpsichord.
Six charity children from the Ospedaletto

* A sequin was worth about 9*s.* 4*d.*—E<small>D</small>.

attiréd in white with Pomegranates in their hair sang music so exquisite and Voluptuous that one lady in the company swooned from excess of pleasure and I will own I was moved to tears. Met a gentleman by name Count Zannetto, an elegant young man in a suit of lemon coloured Melodino. He attached himself to me with ardour, exchanging smiles and glances all evening. A strange, witty devil. Informed me that in his opinion Love should endure the space of a kiss, that he had made love to every woman in Venice, and that his mode of living was Messetto, bassetta, Donnetta.* Then he presented me with his visiting card engraved with a Cupid and declared that he Adored me.

I laughed, and cried he was a Wicked Rake, but I will own I was reluctant to depart when Madame Dupont came for me.

April 18*th*.

Poor unhappy old Signor Dolfino has died of a Rage brought on by a Pert Niece.

Papa declares I shall kill him this way one day. We visited the Ridotto and I laughed to perceive Ned playing at Faro with a Lady

* A little mass, a little gamble, a little lady.—Ed.

with Coal Black Eyes leaning on his shoulder lovingly. Papa did not observe him. Doubtless Ned is running into Debt.

Stefano remarked to me to-day that I was killing the Gondola, I used it so often, and added that 'twas easier to watch a Sack of Fleas than a woman. 'Tis droll to observe how familiar the lower classes are with the Quality in this place.

April 19*th.*

A diverting Marionette Theatre in the Campo San Maurizio this morning. A Sacred procession passed by and all the crowd kneeled, leaving me upright, so I ran into an apothecary's shop and there met face to face my crimson gallant of St. Mark's. He bowed very courteously and escorted me to his Gondola, and thence to the Piazza where we sat and eat an Ice together.

His English as weak as my Italian, so our conversation confined to smiles.

A very genteel young man, and I gave him my lace handkerchief on parting.

A courtezan has her appartements overlooking our parlour. She sits in the window of evenings in a Deshabille très Gallant and

combs her hair, and makes Sheep's eyes at
Ned. Papa very Vexed at this, and pulls
the shutters to with an Oath, to Ned's
chagrin.

April 20th.

Ned and me strolling down the Calle
della Madonetta this evening, when a window
opened and a lady lowered a basket containing, to our amazement, a new born Infant!
This was seized by a Gondolier who wrapped
it in his cloak, sprang into his craft and rowed
off without more to do. A strange City
indeed.

April 22nd.

To-day to Murano to see the Convent.
Invitation sent us by " Sua Eccelenza Abba-
dessa Reverendissima Donna Caterina Princi-
pessa Emos." Ned attired himself sumptuously in gold brocade, for he had heard that
the nuns were excessively pretty, and have
lovers. The convent parlour full of guests
of high degree. The nuns many young and
captivating seated behind a thin grille, wearing low dresses and jewels. Ned plainly
catched by one of them, a creature with

green eyes and blonde curls, who returned his doux yeux lavishly. Saw to my pleasure Count Z., with a party of noble ladies. I told him it was a pity to see so many pretty women behind bars—but he winked and assured me that they had not renounced the affairs of the world, or the Pleasures of Love by any means. He informed me that the famous monsieur Casanova had an affair with a nun in this very convent, ten or more years ago, but was imprisoned in the Leads for all his Licentiousness. Should not be surprised if Count Z. found himself there too. We have moved to appartments at the Regina d'Inghilterra for Papa cannot abide the racket beneath our windows.

April 23rd.

To a party given by some of the noble ladies here. There being only females, and no Gentlemen present, we drank our chocolate on the roof of the palazzo, and several of the guests loosened their hair. This bleaching in the sun they declare produces the auburn tint, for which the Venetian Ladies are so celebrated. One young lady sang to us very sweetly, accompanying herself on the guitar. We foretold the future with cards and exchanged gossip. Apropos of this it would seem that Mr. Houghton is so enamoured of Mme. Dejeune that he pays her four thousand ducats a year to keep her from his rivals. I should not have supposed her worth it, from what I have observed of her in the arcades.

The Contessa M—— cannot it appears retain her lovers because . . .* The ladies threw off all discretion and talked of their own love affairs, most freely. I heard things I could scarcely write down. This is indeed a gallant and loose city. I believe that poor Nanette and self are the only virtuous females in Venice.

April 25th.
I met the gallant in the crimson cloak in the Piazzetta. He begged me most ardently to grant him the favour of a rendezvous to-morrow night. He swears on his Honour that it is to be nothing but a turn up the

* This remark has been deleted as too frank for modern readers. It alludes to a personal defect.—ED.

Grand Canal—which he declares is excessively beautiful by moonlight. He promises that it shall be arranged with utter secrecy, and that Papa shall know nothing of it.

April 27th.

Experienced last night a most Alarming and Terrible Adventure. My Imagination inflamed, and my Prudence overcome by the beauty and balminess of the night and I decided to yield to the request of my Beau. Attired myself in mask and cloak. Stefano, whom I had bribed, unlocked the door for me at midnight. Met my gallant as arranged in the little court behind this place. He embraced me tenderly, and was preparing to lead me to his gondola when the air was rent by a Fearful Scream. There was a Curse, a Splash and a Gurgle, and a gondola sped by us, in the narrow canal—in it a young female struggling for dear life. Perceived by the moonlight, to my Indescrible Horror, the corpse of a young man floating face downwards in the canal! I uttered a Shriek, we heard the sound of running footsteps, whereupon my Friend throwing his cloak over me whispered: "Quick, hasten home," and ran like a hare down the Calle. Thank Heavens, Stefano had the door ajar, and I stumbled into his arms near dead with fright. Revived by a glass of wine, I wept. S. informed me in a low voice that such midnight assassinations are not uncommon here. Thankful to reach my bed and lay awake all night in a tremble. Cannot forget that poor murdered body. No more terrible punishment could I have had for my Indiscretion. I vow I will never more embark on these romantic escapades. Suffered from the Vapours all day.

April 29th.

Poor Nanette is sick of the Colic. The foolish wretch had a pain in her head, and purchased a remedy from a quack doctor in the Piazza—and this is the result.

Apropos of Ills. I am astounded to see how sensitive the Venetian Ladies are to odours of all kinds. It appears that Mme F. swooned this morning on account of a smell of frying, which penetrated from her kitchen to her chamber.

April 30th.

It would appear that this town is bristling with spies. Ned finds that the little ballerina he has been conducting an intrigue with, is in the pay of the French. He has repented of his penchant on hearing this, and deserted her. Papa commends him highly for his discretion. Ned has also heard that the dead body of a priest yesterday night was found in a well near the Friari. It seems that such tragedies take place daily. Papa however declares that he has heard that the Inquisitors have but one spy. I recollect now being informed that the Comtessa P. was accused last month of having poisoned an Aged Husband and was soon after found stabbed in her bed. Some say this is an act of Vengeance. At all event very shocking. To a party where we played cards on a rug.

May 1st.

Great rejoicings to-day. The Doge presented a bouquet of flowers to San Giorgio Maggiore. Ned and me watched the procession from the balcony. The road illuminated by torches, and the Dalmatian bodyguard sounded their trumpets.

May 3rd.

A fine regatta to-day on the Grand Canal. The gondolas all decked out with flowers and brocade.

There was a race of boats—sometimes females take part in these races. Many of the larger vessels magnificent as various symbolical objects, such as the Chariot of Juno, the Chariot of the Stars, the Kingdom of France, the Chariot of Love and so on. The gondoliers in superb habits. It seems that the State wish to suppress all this extravagance, and richness of attire on the part of the nobles, but these sumptuary laws have little effect, I believe. Justina Conti declares that there is an edict against false bosoms. These are imported from France, and are much in vogue among the slighter Venetian Ladies. The lower classes attire themselves richly here on festive occasions. The women wear skirts and bodices of bright hues, white slippers, gold chains and pretty ribbons.

The bourgeosie it seems are more sober in their costume and manner of living. To-day I went to the Rialto where all the merchants live. 'Tis a very busy industrious place, and stinks of tan. Purchased a fine water melon from a brown naked child.

May 5th.

Papa and me dined to-day with old Signor Nani. His palazzo is sumptuous. He possesses a fine library, and many beautiful antiques. We were surprised to observe a bust of Shakespeare, and it seems that our host is a prodigious admirer of the immortal Bard. We dined in a summer-house on the roof garden—the smallest plot of ground imaginable, but half the dimensions of the rose garden at Kearney. Signor N. monstrously vain of it.

It was so encumbered with antiques that it was near impossible to move about. One statue of Aphrodite very pleasing.

The conversation lively and witty, but the meal itself very frugal, as I have observed before now at Venetian parties. Signor Nani has recently printed, at his own expense, the works of Ovid. All the Venetians penning books, pamphlets and poems vigourously. The talk is all of the struggle between the nobles and the Ten, whom it seems are Tyrannical. Signor N. says 'tis easy for an enemy to slip a note of accusation in the Lion's mouth, and so bring about one's arrest. He informed us that the Nobles are ruining themselves at the Ridotto. One, the other day, staked all his garments, and had to return home naked. The Bourgeois assume the dress of Nobles, all of every rank are as dissolute as they can be, the zentildonne are nothing but courtezans, in short he was full of complaints.

We drank coffee, played cards, and heard music. Signor Nani presented me with an exquisite fan painted by Rosalba Carriera.*

May 6th.

Conte Z. to-day asked me to become his mistress. Informed me that he had a sumptously furnished casetta waiting for me. Upon my refusing the honour he seemed very put out, and declared that Englishwomen were as cold as Dead Fishes. I informed him that I was enamoured of another man, whereupon he left me in a rage, crying that he had never been treated in such a way before.

May 9th.

A prodigiously tiresome to do to-day.

* Well-known Venetian artist.—ED.

Nanette came to me weeping and at length confessed that she had been seduced by that villainous gondolier Stefano, though why she should think it necessary to inform me of this Heaven knows. She wailed and vowed that she would never have left her beloved land had she known what a Licentious place I was bringing her to. Fear I scolded her somewhat sharply, for I cannot comprehend why such a Plain wench should not be virtuous. Papa heard the traccasserie, came to inquire the reason and flew into a fearful passion calling her a wanton, and every rude name imaginable, at which she wept the louder. Papa summoned Stefano and damned him furiously. The wretch had the Barefacedness to declare that such a clumsy girl should be thankful any man had looked Twice at her. At length I turned the whole crew out of my chamber and bolted the door.

The household has been thrown into confusion by this odious occurrence. The porter, father to Stefano, fell upon his son and beat him with a stick. Papa curses the Venetians and the sex in general.

Met Conte Z. buying tarts in the Piazza.

He bowed to me, not in the least abashed. Laughed heartily when I informed him of this business, and said 'twas only to be expected. Fear he has a wagging tongue, for hardly had we parted than half a dozen of my acquaintances asked me if 'twas true our gondolier had seduced my waiting maid. Am weary of the whole affair.

May 11th.

Stefano and Nanette wedded to-day at the Parish church of San Moise. Papa determined on this union, and the gondolier's tears and entreaties would not move him. Gave Nanette my flowered silk for the ceremony. I vow 'twas the most melancholy affair of the kind I have attended. The bride weeping with shame, the bridegroom very sullen. Happily, Nanette is a native of the Papist canton of Valais, so they are of the same Faith.

Many of Stefano's relatives and friends present, and they laughed and chattered throughout the ceremony as if they were at the play.

Stefano regained his natural liveliness of spirits somewhat after the nuptial repast, which we had spread for them, and informed me that though Nanette was plain she was well covered, and would doubtless prove a good housewife.　Have doubts if this marriage will prove very felicitous, more especially as I have observed that some of the lower class Venetian females are excessively handsome, but Papa takes great merit to himself for having made " one female at all events Respectable."

May 12*th.*

To-day have attained my 21st year.　Papa presents me with an elegant rose satin cloak embroidered with golden butterflies, such as the Ladies wear here, a black mask edged with fine lace, and a pair of embroidered gloves, all this in preparation for the Carnival. Also he has given me a sumptuously bound copy of Goldoni's comedies, which I cannot read yet, but which I shall treasure as a proof of Papa's Esteem and Affection.　Ned absent these last few days, and my father is very Vexed at him not being present for this Anniversary.　Papa and self had a very touching interview this morning.　Papa pleased to say that I have been a more Dutiful

Daughter of late, and I for my part vowed not to vex him any more. Apropos of Sentiment I am wondering if Mr. Ancaster is thinking of me to-day, or if he has been False enough to forget the day of my Birth. I will own I am Mortified at having no word from him. If he could but know I have not thought of him overmuch of late, not from any inconstancy, but from the great Bustle I have been in. The days pass here in a most agreeable trivial manner. Have not opened a book or lifted a needle for weeks. The mornings I shop in the Merceria, drink chocolate and gossip; afternoons, visits and gossip; evenings, parties or trips in the gondola, and more gossip again. Scandal and talk of clothes occupies my time. Am continually running around to see the sights. I wear out a pair of slippers in a week here. Never have I been more light-hearted, and I vow I shall be monstrously sad to leave for Vienna.

Conte Z. sent me a lovely bouquet of flowers to-day with the inscription: " To my Virtous but ever adored Cleonetta."

Several of my acquaintances have brought me little gifts.

Lucrezia Reni was malicious enough to say " What, 21 and not yet married!" Papa also mentioned that he had received a letter from Mr. Sutcliffe who hoped to pay his respects to me on our return.

Lucrezia Reni declares that Madame Maria Gla——go has given birth to a monster. I could scarce believe this, but she swears 'tis correct. Her maid was informed of it from the maid of the lady's sister. This woman declares she helped to tie it in a sack and throw it in the Canal. Could anything be more shocking ?

May 16th.—*Feast of the Ascension.*

All Venice En Fête to-day, from earliest dawn for the Festival of the Betrothal of the Adriatic. Was woken up at 4 by singing and shouting below my window. Papa and me and Ned attired ourselves in our gayest garments. Had vast difficulty in making our way to the Gradinigos palace, the Canal so thronged with craft. Partook of a light repast with our hosts and entered one of their gondolas in which they had been aimable enough to allow us places. Thus we had an excellent view all day of the Festivities. The G.s' gondola draped superbly in gold brocade, fringed with purple, their ladder embroidered in silver upon either side. Their gondoliers in rich costumes, the oars gilded. I lay on cushions of purple satin and thanked heaven I had on my Lilac satin and Pearls for this Festive occasion. We made our way laboriously in the wake of the Bucentaur, which is a superb gilded state vessel, and had the satisfaction of seeing the Doge perform the Ceremony though from a distance. The water covered with craft of all kind, War-ships and merchantships decked in flags, gondolas, feluccas, galleys and skifs. Indeed, I believe, one might have walked to the Lido over the water without wetting a shoe buckle by stepping from boat to boat. The finest day possible. Bells ringing and tapestry hung from all the windows. I swear I was utterly confused by the brilliance of the scene, and Papa declares he has never in all his life seen anything so fine. Everyway was a field of jewels, brocade, flowers, pearls, and fans. An incessant noise of music and cries from the gondoliers. Numerous quarrels and heads were broken.

A banquet given by the Doge in the Palace. A table laid with rare fruits, sweets and wax ornaments. The mob admitted to this in masks. Ned and me with a great crowd of people waited to see the marvellous clock on the Tower. On the stroke of the hour a door opened by the Madonna's Throne, and a procession of angels and wise men came out walking like live people. Never have I seen anything so ingenious and cunning. I cannot think how 'tis done.

To bed now vastly late, my head in a buz.

May 17*th*.

Carnival commenced yesterday and this place is gone Mad. All masked from the Doge to Stephano and every vestige of Discretion thrown aside. The city is in an uproar. All work is at an end. Day and night equally Lively, and cafés open from dawn to dawn. My pen cannot describe the License and Jollity which reigns. Papa, in view of the general confusion, ordered me sternly to keep within doors unless escorted by Nanette or a domestic, but there is no

such thing as Rule or order now, and I slipped
on a cloak and mask over male attire (breeches
and coat of rose satin and sulphur waistcoat)
climbed down the balcony into a gondola,
and so away ! 'Twould keep me up all night
if I were to note down all the curious sights
I have seen.

The Piazza is filled with booths and stalls
and high poles with banners, and a crowd so
thick that I was near pressed to death. I vow
there must be thousands of foreigners now
in Venice. A mass of singers, acrobats,
fortune tellers, dancers and clowns. Saw a
panther and an elephant by the Ducal
Palace, and to my vast amazement an Irish
dwarf (or so they called him) for when I asked
him what county he came from he could not
comprehend a word! 'Tis as well my morals
are not as loose as poor Nanette's, for I could
have found occasion to-day for a score of
Amorous Adventures. A quantity of Mas-
queraders begged me to enter their gondolas,
and my arm has been pinched and pulled
till it is Black and Blue. Kisses are plentiful
but the Mask is mighty convenient, for it
does away with the need to blush. Took me

an hour to return from the Piazza to this place. Experienced some odious little adventures, and was constrained to draw my little dagger now and again.

May 18*th.*

Ned and me to the play. A ballet and the dancers threw themselves into strange contortions. The town lighted by lanterns and gay ribbons stretched from house to house.

To a party at the Testas. We proceeded round the town in Gondolas hung with jessamine, and singing barcarolles and serenades. This gaiety lasts for 2 weeks. I swear I shall be worn to a Shred by the finish, for 'tis near impossible to snatch a Wink of Sleep at night, with all the sounds of Merrymaking.

May 20*th.*

'Tis damnably hot now and I feel somewhat in a fever what with all the Buz and Racket of these last few days.

Last night tossing on my couch, I could have sworn I heard a familiar voice singing beneath my window. Ran onto the balcony but saw nothing but a gondola rowed by a tall masked figure, passing by in the light of the moon.

'Tis Droll what strange tricks an over-heated Fancy will play upon the Mind! Ned away once more. Papa declares this town is like a Madhouse.

May 21*st*.

Il Travestito has commenced. Even my father owns 'tis diverting to observe the various costumes. 'Tis indeed enough to make one split to see them. Saw to-day in the Piazza a Bear on a Wooden Horse, a Devil and an Archangel all in a few seconds! Anything however droll will serve as a disguise, a Pig's head or a pillow case worn on the head. Some of the females wear moustaches, while the men garb themselves as courtezans, old women and so on. Watched a tight rope dance in the Piazza. We met Conte Z. attired as an Ape. He informed us that one year a patrician Lady performed on the rope in the Public Gaze. We pur-chased biscuits and fruit from a hawker. To an assembly at the Crimani. Attired myself as Hebe. Some monstrous tasteful rich costumes.

May 22nd.

A Most Terrible Catastrophe has fallen
on us! My hand trembles so with Indignation that I can scarce pen these words. No
more frightful contretemps has occurred to
us on these Travels, and I feel deeply the
need for some Sympathetic Female to whom
I could confide my Fears and failing such a
person I must again Fly to my faithful
Journal. Am Thankful poor Dear Mama is
in Heaven and not able to see the Disgrace
her favorite child has brought upon us.

In short that Damnable Intolerable Fool
Ned has run off with a Nun ! It seems that
he has been conducting an intrigue with her
for some weeks, indeed since he first set eyes
upon her that day at Murano. Yesterday
with Unpardonable Foolishness he attempted
to elope with his Flame. The Baggage
escaped from her cell, and the 2 wretches took
gondola to the mainland and so hoped to
fly to Geneva and be married. Their flight
was apprehended, they were pursued by the
lady's relatives and overtaken. She has been
flung once more into her Convent and poor

Rash Ned has been arrested by order of the counsil and is under lock and key.

Our first intimation of this horrible business was this morning when to my Alarm a party of State Officers entered the house and conducted a search of Ned's room. Papa was away, and I thus learnt of the alarming fate which has overtaken my Unhappy brother. They departed after having sealed the escritoire, and all Ned's boxes. My father found me weeping on the ground amid Ned's scattered garments. Informed of the disaster he unlaced my dress and administered Smelling Salts with touching Solicitude, and hastened away by Gondola to the British Ambassador.

He has not yet returned and I am in a Terrible Tremble. Gracious Heavens, why did not Ned's inclination lead him to ballet dancers and courtezans? Sure there are enough loose women in Venice if he must be dissolute, without him ravishing a Cloistered Nun.

It would appear that what renders his crime more grave is that his love who is but 14, is a member of one of the highest

Venetian families and a daughter of the
Golden Book. I swear I dare not write the
name in this book so illustrious is it, and there
is every possibility that our belongings may
be again subjected to search. Indeed I mean
to keep this Journal under my mattress or
in some safe place, lest an indiscrete remark
in it should lead to my arrest. Stefano declares we shall be now under the scrutiny of
the Inquisitors' spies day and night, and
counsels me to keep within doors.

What seems to me so strange in this affair
is that if Ned had merely continued to be the
lover of this Nun all would have been well,
for they are permitted to carry on intrigues
and lead lives of great immorality; but to
attempt to become her lawful husband was
it seems an Unpardonable Sin, and thus poor
Ned is to suffer for the first Respectable thing
I have ever known him do! The lady in
question is an heiress whose wealth the convent doubtless expects to inherit, and this I
fear will make their vengeance upon Ned
the more Ferocious. As for her Papist
relatives 'tis plain that her crime in their
eyes lies in her having brought open scandal

upon them in attempting to wed a foreign heretic.

A small crowd has been around this house since the dreaded Inquisitors' gondola was here this morning, and 'tis enough to keep me indoors, for in my present condition of Agitation I have not the Courage to subject myself to the Laughter and Remarks of a Venetian crowd. Lud! I am too weary to write a word more.

May 23rd.

We are still in the Deepest anxiety with regard to the unhappy Ned. Papa is at our minister's day and night now. We are highly apprehensive lest poor Ned should be confined for months in the State Prison, like poor Monsieur de Briand who was 10 months in dungeon below water, and was released only to expire of a slow fever. Papa says at the best we shall be obliged to pay immense sums to obtain his release.

The news of his escapade has spread all over Venice. Many of our acquaintances including the Manins, the Loredans and the Bonfadinis have called on me to-day to satisfy their Curiosity and express their

Condolences. Most are Affable and Solicitous but one or 2 were excessively spiteful, in
particular Lucrezia Reni and Maddalena
Sarbellon. Indeed I'll own my Deepest
Shame arises from the fact that a member of
my family should have repaid the hospitality
offered us here in such a Base manner.

It seems that Signor S—— who is a member
of the Senate and was so agreeable to us at
the Rout at the Barbaro, promises to assist us
with regard to Ned.

May 24th
Papa interviewed to-day the father of
Ned's charmer. He returned deeply dejected and informed me that her relatives
are enraged, and determined to avenge themselves upon Ned. Papa is making fresh
efforts with our English minister.

Paddy in a great Melancholy. He has
ceased cursing Stefano and tells his beads all
day long now.

May 25th.
At the Ambassador's intercession Ned has
been moved to a larger cell, and I was permitted the melancholy Pleasure of sending

him a few necessities. He sent a message begging for some clean linen and books. Madame Dupont and me prepared a box containing the same, and I added some pastries, a flask of wine, a snuff box and one or two lively novels which I pray may cheer the unhappy reprobate.

Also sent pen and paper with which he is to write a full Confession, to lay before his Judges at his examination. 'Tis a thousand pities I cannot write this for him, for his Style is very halting.

The Carnival continues with unabated Vigour but I, needless to say, take no part in it. Would to Heaven it were over, for the incessant racket drives me near Frantic.

May 26th.

Papa saw Ned to-day. The poor youth he reports as being Deeply Dejected.

Signor N. has had the goodness to counsel my father to wait upon Madame Margherita Trami, the mistress of a Most Important Personage. This woman, he declares, if presented with a handsome gift might be more Efficacious in obtaining Ned's relief than all the efforts of our Ambassador.

Papa has a rendezvous with her at her house this evening, and commissioned me to purchase a present got her in the Merceria. Decided on a handsome pair of pearl and enamel earrings, which should excite the creature's cupidity and gratify her Vanity, and so lead to good results.

May 27th.

To-day the Inquisitors sit upon Ned. We are in a Terrible To Do. 'Tis now four o'clock and no news has been heard, though Papa, Paddy and Stephano are waiting in the Antechamber. Lord help us !

May 28th.

Heaven be blessed ! Ned is to be released and will be returned to us in about 5 days. Papa and me on hearing the Joyous Tidings near wept with Pleasure !

'Tis indeed delightful to feel that our Tribulations are at an end, and that the poor wretch will soon be at Liberty.

'Twas late last night that Paddy and Stephano returned post haste with the glad news. Papa and Signor Nani later. Papa is to pay £200 in sequins to the injured parents, and £150 to the convent. Ned's unhappy flame is to do penance. Shall pass a Calm Night at length. Monstrous relief. Great rejoicings in the .household ! Paddy ceased telling his beads and renews his swearing at Stefano. Papa says we must leave for Vienna the very day Ned is freed, lest the relatives of the nun, who are still Indignant, should wreak some vengeance upon him.

Must interview Rosina apropos of a Travelling Gown.

I must not only put up my own belongings but also overlook the packing of Ned's wardrobe.

May 29th.

Stupendous Discovery ! Mr. A. is in Venice.

ENVOI

Miss Cleone Elizabeth Knox's Journal ends abruptly here. Fortunately, I have been able to trace her subsequent movements from a voluminous correspondence which has been preserved in Ned Knox's family, and is still in the possession of his descendants.

Mr. David Ancaster had evidently left Ireland some months previously on account of a duelling escapade, and had been travelling on the Continent with Sir James Ford. He had arrived at Lausanne on his way to Rome, and hearing there of the movements of the Knox family, had left his companion and followed them to Venice.

There, as seen in the Journal, he got into communication with Miss Knox. A tradition in the Knox family is that he made his presence known to her by singing an Irish ballad under her window.

The lovers decided to elope before Cleone was taken away to Vienna by her father, and five days after the last entry (June 3rd) they left Venice together, taking with them Nanette, the maid, her husband, Stefano Scomparine, and the dog Chloe.

R

Miss Knox, one gathers from a letter written to her some weeks later by her brother Ned, left most of her personal belongings behind, including her journal. Ned Knox promises to send her " your beloved Diary," but he probably never did so, for it was rediscovered in 1904 among the Knox family documents.

Old Mr. Knox, as would be expected, was very angry at his daughter's action. The state of mind he was in can be deduced from answers to letters of his written to various members of his family.

Tom Foley, his son-in-law, sends from Derbyshire four closely-written pages of condolence.

" Cary and me," he writes, " are more Agitated and Distressed than we can say at this unforeseen Catastrophe. We beg you, dear sir, to calm your Outraged Paternal Feelings, and put your trust in Heaven, who in its Goodness will surely not permit our beloved sister to be utterly ruined by that Scoundrel Ancaster."

He also confesses that he and his wife had always felt doubtful as to the advisability

of exposing " a young female of C.'s lively
disposition to the Temptations of the continent." The fears which Mr. Knox and
his family evidently felt were fortunately
groundless.

Mr. David Ancaster and Miss Cleone Knox
were married ten days after they left Venice,
in the Protestant church at Geneva, by Pastor
Getay.

From Switzerland they left for Paris,
where they remained a fortnight with Madame
de Brinoy de Chateauroux. A letter of hers
to Mr. Knox, written, no doubt, at Cleone's
instigation, assures him that "*vos chers
enfants sont follement heureux*" and begs him
to forgive them.

This letter is addressed to Vienna. In
spite of the elopement, Mr. Knox and his
son do not seem to have altered their plans
for their Grand Tour. The young couple
then returned to London, where they awaited
Mr. Knox's return. Unfortunately, no description has been found of the interview
between Mr. Knox and his new son-in-law.
There are various other letters written at this

time and relating to the episode. Three are from Mr. Knox's lawyer in London on the subject of Cleone's fortune, and pointing out to Mr. Knox that he could not prevent her enjoying it now that she was of age.

There is also another letter from Tom Foley, thanking his father-in-law for the copy of Cleone and David Ancaster's marriage certificate, and a facetious one from Cousin Noll, who is mentioned in the journal and who was Mr. Oliver Knox of Ballywiticock House.

Mr. and Mrs. David Ancaster returned to Ireland in the spring of 1766 and settled down at Castle Ancaster, Co. Down. The relations between the two families seem to have been rather strained at first, but after Cleone had presented old Mr. Knox with two grandsons, he evidently became completely reconciled to her and her husband.

Ned Knox married in 1769 Miss Bullen, an heiress, and Cleone Ancaster stood as god-mother to his first child.

Cleone Ancaster herself had 12 children, eight of whom were boys and four girls.

Contrary, no doubt, to general expectation, the long married life of David and Cleone Ancaster appears to have been extremely happy and prosperous.